THE LAST
SANE WOMAN

THE LAST
SANE WOMAN

A Novel

by Hannah Regel

VERSO
London • New York

First published by Verso 2024
© Hannah Regel 2024

1 3 5 7 9 10 8 6 4 2

Verso
UK: 6 Meard Street, London W1F 0EG
US: 388 Atlantic Avenue, Brooklyn, NY 11217
versobooks.com

Verso is the imprint of New Left Books

ISBN-13: 978-1-80429-537-3
ISBN-13: 978-1-80429-539-7 (US EBK)
ISBN-13: 978-1-80429-538-0 (UK EBK)

British Library Cataloguing in Publication Data
A catalogue record for this book is available from the British Library

Library of Congress Cataloging-in-Publication Data

Names: Regel, Hannah, author.
Title: The last sane woman : a novel / by Hannah Regel.
Description: London ; New York : Verso, 2024.
Identifiers: LCCN 2023053675 (print) | LCCN 2023053676 (ebook) | ISBN
   9781804295373 (paperback) | ISBN 9781804295397 (ebk) | ISBN
   9781804295380 (UK ebk)
Subjects: LCGFT: Novels.
Classification: LCC PR6118.E5865 L37 2024 (print) | LCC PR6118.E5865
   (ebook) | DDC 823/.92 – dc23/eng/20231204
LC record available at https://lccn.loc.gov/2023053675
LC ebook record available at https://lccn.loc.gov/2023053676

Typeset in Elektra by Biblichor Ltd, Scotland
Printed and bound by CPI Group (UK) Ltd, Croydon, CR0 4YY

For my mum, Sharon.

The Last
Sane Woman

A NOVEL

Hannah
Regel

The smell is lost. She can get it sometimes, but only when it comes to her unasked, like music, on the whiff of certain detergents or a meal being cooked. There is light, though. It falls in a big sloping square on the floor where the cat would sit. Does sit. In her memory two little girls are crouched on the floor talking to it. The cat enjoys the sun as only cats can do, oblivious to their quiet mutterings.

'I love it so much I want to throw it out the window,' says one.

'I know what you mean,' says the other, squeezing its tail.

1

'I want to read about women who can't make things.'

'I'm not sure I understand?' said Marcella Goodwoman, raising a hand to adjust her crocodile clip and gathering the thin grey hairs that had fallen to her neck. A stack of pink cardboard document folders teetered behind her. In a far corner, peeling paint shimmered in the steam above a recently boiled kettle.

On her way to the Feminist Assembly, Nicola Long had worked on this request, rephrasing it in her head until the sentiment felt correct. Now she'd said it aloud, she could hear how vague it sounded. That morning, watching a child attempt to blow bubbles from a tube for the first time, it had made perfect sense. I want you to blow me some bubbles, she had said in her kindest voice. I want you to be happy, I want you to know how. You dip the wand in the liquid, take it out carefully and blow. No, not like that. That's too fast. No, you're holding it too tight. If you tilt it, it will spill. No, not on the carpet. You have to blow outwards, like this. Not in your mouth, please don't eat it, not rough like that, not upside down or in your eye, not with two hands it will fall. No, you're not listening. You are doing it wrong, you are using it wrong. Stop.

Marcella finished with her clip and set her hands patiently on her lap, waiting for an explanation.

'I want to read about the trouble a person might have with making things. About what might stop a person from making things, making art, I mean. Like money,' Nicola added, 'or time.'

Doubt.

'Yes. I see. We have a scroll from a Gazelle workshop at the Tate Modern.' Marcella got up from her chair and left the room to enter the archive's store. She returned some minutes later carrying a heavy reel of paper.

'It was laid out as a tablecloth,' she explained as she unrolled it onto the cramped central desk in the reading room, 'Everyone invited sat down, took up a pen, and wrote out what had stopped them from working.'

The paper tablecloth had the words 'money' and 'children' written on it again and again in thick black marker.

'What kind of artists were they at the table?'

'Mostly organisers, educators.'

No good, thought Nicola. Too proactive. She wanted to wallow, and this seemed like too much of an exercise in trying to live.

'No, it needs to be about objects. About women who can't make *things*.' She wanted the blunt difficulty of being faced with a mass. When she said the word *things* she took her phone from the back pocket of her jeans and knocked it against the desk. Marcella moved her head to show she

4

had understood and was rethinking, then began to roll the tablecloth back up. It was covered in post-it notes that elaborated on the words 'money' and 'children' and they were coming unstuck as she fumbled, their glue diminished from the years.

'Okay. Now, let's think . . . There are the letters,' Marcella said before wandering off again. A post-it note with the word 'debt' written on it had found its way onto her calf. Nicola watched it wiggle away. Marcella returned, struggling this time with a large cardboard archival box. Grey, roughly a metre squared, and seven or so inches deep.

'Sensitive material,' she said, lowering her voice, 'I only show the letters to people I know the F. A. can trust.'

Nicola beamed inwardly at the flattery. This was the first time they had met, and after the tablecloth's unrolling and rerolling, she felt she had been a nuisance. But apparently not. She straightened her back and nodded as solemnly as she could to show she was, as assumed, trustworthy. Was she not, after all, a woman, standing in an archive dedicated to women's art? She was present, and therefore good.

'It's difficult, you see, because of her death. When she was alive she was a ceramicist, a potter.'

Nicola was interested now. With her thumb she pushed up the lid of the box, now set between them in one of the light wood study carrels that lined the room's edge. It was crammed full of envelopes. Why because of her death? Nicola was about to ask, but Marcella went on speaking.

'She took her own life. They were donated to us after she died by the woman she was writing to. It's all one-sided, here.' Marcella then leant around Nicola to make a gap between the tightly packed envelopes with two fingers. She repeated this gesture several times to show that the addressee was the same on each one: Susan, Susan, Susan, Susan.

'You have until six.'

Marcella left Nicola alone and returned to her office at the other end of the narrow room, shutting the door behind her.

Nicola lifted the lid. Inside were hundreds of envelopes organised in bundles and tied together with string. Each bundle must have held at least thirty letters and had a small card marker wedged into it with the year stamped on: 1976, 1977, 1978, and so on, until they stopped at 1988. This was *stationery* stationery: pastel envelopes with floral designs, foliage and sunset stripes. Pink and cream and pasty yellow. They seemed almost to giggle, inside their stale grey box. Nicola lifted out the first envelope, which was the colour of blush, and turned it over in her hand. Then she put it down on the desk and stared. She recognised the address: 42 Dewfield Road, Basford, Nottingham. Not precisely, not the exact house, but she knew it. She could picture the hazy red bricks and the squat, raised front lawns, sprouting weeds. It was not far from where she'd been born, and where her mother, a dentist's assistant nearing sixty, still lived. She pulled the letter out with quick fingers and began to read.

Dear Susan,

I found the most beautiful letter set at the craft market and couldn't resist, even though I don't really have anyone to write to. Everyone I know I could practically summon with a tin can. But then I thought to myself, what about Susan? You're far enough away. So, here we are. You better be game and write back! I will ask you lots of flattering questions so you have to. I want this to go on forever and then when we're very, very old we can look back on it and read about all the men we've eaten and forgotten and you'll thank me for having such a good idea!

I know I saw you for your birthday, but what about after . . . any changes? Twenty-one, eh?

Nicola did some rough arithmetic. Assuming she was still alive, Susan would be her mother's age, give or take a few years. But the other woman, the other woman did not live, which would make her Nicola's.

'I like her,' Nicola said as she helped Marcella carry the letters back into the store after being summoned at six o'clock, 'I really like . . .' She was stopped by the fact that despite spending a long afternoon of parties and boyfriends and late period scares with her, she did not know the potter's name, who signed off only with *love*, or a kiss. Nicola hadn't noticed before, but she saw now that the name on the box was Susan Baddeley. The Susan Baddeley Papers. Odd, she thought. Surely they belong to the potter? But then she supposed not.

7

'Oh, I'm glad, dear. She's been here for so long, it's about time someone paid her some attention.' Marcella spoke about the potter as if the box and its contents were her person. When Nicola asked her name, Marcella looked up at the ceiling and paused dramatically.

'No, sorry, it's gone. I did know it. Age, unfortunately. Terrible thing. If you want to carry on reading them,' she continued, 'you can put your name down here to reserve them.'

She pointed to a weekly diary which, like everything else in the archive – the caramel-coloured filing cabinets, the waxed wooden desks – looked tragically old-fashioned. A slither of red ribbon kept the diary in time. Marcella ran her wrist along the centre fold so that it stayed open on her desk. Once it was flattened between them she explained to Nicola how it worked.

'You write your name down here, and the resource you want to look at, here. If someone has written their name and the name of what you'd like to look at on a particular day, then you'll have to pick another time to come in. If you want something urgently, it's usually best to plan ahead.'

Nicola looked down at the analogue week. There were no other names.

'Done,' she said, pointing to where she had written her name next to Susan Baddeley's for the remaining weekdays.

'OK,' squinting, 'Nicola. See you tomorrow.'

'Is it very sad?'

'I'm sorry?'

'Is it very sad when she dies?'

'I haven't read them, dear. You'll have to tell me.'

Nicola liked her too, Marcella. She had a way about her, a way like maybe she did know. Nicola was glad she didn't tell. She didn't want the potter to die, at least not yet, not like that: conversationally. She wanted to keep coming back.

2

The children are watching a Punch and Judy show in the rain. Donna Dreeman swerves to avoid them, darting in and out of shoppers. The thud of Punch's club against Judy's head in time with her steps. Knock, knock, knock.

That's the way to do it!

Rounding her eyes upward to acknowledge the deluge, she shares a sigh with the woman whose stall she's found herself under.

'Those won't do you much good in this,' the stall-keeper says. Donna's boots, cracked across the throat line of each foot, look like something spat up from the sea. 'No, no good at all. Traditional Gibson clogs. These are what you need. Straight from the factory in Lancashire. Very fashionable on a young girl like you.'

Pushing them forward.

Donna accepts the offering, rubbing her fingers along the stitching. They look well made, she thinks. Bold. Bright red leather with shiny black laces and thick wooden soles. Water seeps persuasively through a sock. She does need better shoes, and tonight *is* an important night. It would be good to wear something nice, something new.

'How much?'

Too much. As Donna makes to turn away, the image of Rose Hayden falls into view. Rose would buy them. Rose would look very distinctive in them. Will look very distinctive, as she always does, tonight. The image of Rose leans against a wall, tosses its hair back and lights a cigarette, turning one heel out in slow, convincing red tap. Competition is a firm hand. As if racing against an approaching landslide, Donna hands over every penny she has.

Watching her money disappear into the tin safe, she's reminded of the rainy lunchtimes of her childhood. Kept inside the classroom to avoid getting wet, she and Susan Bloom would push the small bookcase against the wall to form it, their shop, where they would exchange their scalloped cardigans and gingham-trim ankle socks back and forth for imagined money, dropping buttons into jars and rattling their takings. Funny, she thinks. How you can forget about a person entirely and then up they pop, perfectly formed, for seemingly no reason at all. Mrs Butler. Exasperated by the muddling of clothes, horrified when Susan, low on buttons, takes off her knickers and declares it Daylight Robbery. She remembers sitting on Mrs Butler's carpet, cross-legged, studying the line of blackheads at the crease of her nose while she spoke, and the private vow she had made to herself there: that when she grew up she would never allow herself to be as ugly as Mrs Butler.

11

The bubble of her thoughts bursts with a shove as the stall-keeper hands back the clogs, wrapped in brown paper.

'Have a lovely evening,' waving her off.

Her heartbeat applauds as she ventures back out into the downpour: knock, knock, knock, with the force of an impulse acted upon. That's the way to do it! In gardens and yards beyond the shop fronts, housewives rush from their back doors to tug the sheets down from the line. Umbrellas, like a smack of jellyfish, turn inside-out en masse. Donna pulls her purchase under her coat and heads back home, back past the children and the gaping fish, onion skins, wooden crates and all the other women. All the women, searching for shoes in the rain. Long dark hair swishes past with appalling ease, a softly bent nose with freckles and elegant curls, putting porridge-coloured mittens on a toddler saying shhh, shhhh, another steadies a bike with her free hand, adept, a ponytail bounces, then bangles, a blunt fringe, rollers, hoops, two teenage girls with a mean secret, a mangy cat.

As she manoeuvres through the crowd the landslide she had so narrowly avoided catches her up. It makes its break beneath her ribs. The trees tumble down onto her stomach, wailing from their uptorn roots as they go, crashing down in great tangled balls of earth and bone and string. Spinning brown wires, grasping in the mud-speed, asking:

What kind of a person wears Traditional Gibson Clogs?

The question buries her in dirt.

Standing in the market, covered in mud, she can no longer say what she looks like. She tries to wipe it off, the dirt she thought would never touch her, but every woman who passes heaps a fresh shovel of it on. Rose Hayden returns, this time in purple platforms. Silly, silly, haven't you heard? Red, she says, shaking her head, is dead! A crocodile comes for Judy and the children scream. Against the eruption of small frights she drops the shoes. They land, toppling from the curb with a pitiful roll to rest in the eye of a puddle. Water overtakes the brown paper, turning it black.

She returns to number twelve Bambury Avenue empty-handed. Entering, she finds Helen Robinson in a brightly knit scarf and hat, kneeling on their living-room floor, rehousing a cheese plant.

'Get everything done?' Helen asks.

Because she is empty-handed, there is no need to tell Helen about the clogs in the gutter or the landslide beneath her ribs. She had simply gone to the bank before her important night, and now she had returned.

'Ready?'

'Nearly finished. I thought we could have a drink here before I drive us over. Rose has already left.'

They arrive at a cold room with high ceilings off an alley on the Uttoxeter Road. The room has been reserved for recent graduates in ceramics from North Staffordshire Polytechnic to show their work, and Donna is one of them. Everything she has made for the occasion is arranged evenly throughout the room, with each object on its own wooden plinth. The selection consists of functional wares, bulb-like vases and tapered jugs, all of which could loosely be placed under the bracket of 'pot'. Each pot is slight, like the soft hole in a baby's head. Hand-built and burnished, not glazed. The clay, in its leather-green state, having been rubbed into a radiance with the back of a spoon. She is proud of them. They have a silence that seems to come from somewhere far beyond her. Beyond her own life of red clogs and small frights. She almost can't believe it was she that made them; she that produced something so brave and still. So perfect. As perfect as an egg.

Coloured beads balancing on large breasts, Belinda, her former lecturer, comes bounding over. Belinda's heavily ringed fingers make a big show of batting her hair out the way before leaning in for a continental kiss. Fuss, fuss, fuss. Belinda loves to make a fuss of her, and Donna can feel her skin beginning to flare in response. Blood spreads from her cheeks to her neck in disobedient, crimson blotches. It makes her feel as though she cannot look at Belinda directly, that if she did some secret part of her might be seen, understood, and then snatched.

'Don't pull on that, dear,' Belinda says, swatting Donna's hand away from a button she'd been worrying on her cardigan, before explaining that she has the names for the exhibition dinner – a standing buffet in Belinda's living room, where interested parties will be subjected to an attempted seduction over Mateus Rosé and various purées on crackers. Here are the graduates: lift them up.

'Check the list and tell me if I've left anyone out.'

Donna puts her glass down on the windowsill so as to take a better look. She is not yet used to this kind of thing, professionalism, and truthfully there is not a single person on the list she can imagine spending an enjoyable evening with. She cannot throw the feeling that everyone on it, including Belinda herself, would like in some way or another to eat her up whole. And not in the swelling, joyful way that mothers, having dutifully pushed their children out into the world, profess to wanting their chubby feet back inside their mouths. The button she's been fiddling with falls to the floor. Belinda pretends not to notice.

'You forgot Rose.'

Rose Hayden, with long auburn hair and high bossy hip bones, is leaning against the brickwork telling a man in a pink shirt that no, *she* isn't a potter, *she's* a glass blower. Tiny dots of midnight blue from her painted fingernails flash about her face as she gesticulates. Spotting the shape of her friend at her side, Rose turns to make two three.

'We were just talking about you. I was saying there's no going back. Not like with glass. You can't melt it down and remake it. If *you* change your mind, all it's good for is rubble. I couldn't do it, is what I was saying. So permanent. Do you have a light?'

'Only if you never say rubble again.'

'Rubble. Rubble. Don't be so superstitious. You'll sell all of them, I know it.'

Donna is suddenly not so sure. The clogs creep back into her vision from the gutter; tiny little gnomes are tap-dancing in them. Their dance is a cruel one, mad and fast, with clicking-bent elbows and hunched backs.

Their tongues hang out of their mouths, long and pink and mean.

'Anyway,' Rose goes on, unaware of the commotion, 'I've been listening and I've heard things. Kevin thinks Lizzie Hastings might swing by. Word is she's bringing Richard Reeder and Kevin says if *he* likes you then you're set. Penny Green is his latest, apparently, *if* we're naming names. Are you nervous? Here, have this.'

Rose lifts a small silver hip flask from her handbag and discreetly moves her body to shield her friend while she dips her shoulders to take a swig. The man in the pink shirt leaves them to it.

'You're missing a button by the way.'

Donna tilts her head back and sloshes the vodka into her cheeks. Its heat gives speed to the gnomes who begin to spin. Round and round with each clear and grassy wave, then down her throat. Their smoking bodies tipping head over heels as they fall. Roly, poly, one and then another.

Of course then the evening faded away into a perfect blur of 'really darlings' and 'absolutelys' and 'aren't those interestings'.

A wooden cane taps against the bay window, shimmying rotten splinters of wood onto the carpet. The rot has worn away the frame so that the window is constantly ajar, letting the cold in, even now, in November. It is the kind of cold that stops the blood, so that instead of flowing in fast red lines it crawls. It crawls the veins in shockwaves of traffic, blinking in a weary, yellow way. Lying on the sofa, Donna opens her eyes. Above her head, the damp unfurls its bluish green feathers across the superfresco with a confidence akin to a peacock on heat. A sight for which their landlord's only remedy seems to be that they 'take care to wipe the walls occasionally'. Trevor the landlord who lives next door and is currently standing outside the window.

Walks with a limp, drives a Cortina, eats smoked salmon and Turkish Delight for tea and is altogether outrageous. Dreadful to look at, of course, like a ham in a waistcoat. He is also, always, coming over for what he likes to call INSPECTIONS.

He taps his cane again. She rolls onto a dead arm and pauses for a small while in that place between waking and sleep, lapsing back into an uncertainty of where or when she is, before the cane cracks louder and she is situated exactly by the close damp air and the familiar feeling that the solid rules of the social have once again slipped her grasp. There was nothing funny about a hangover like this. Her brain felt as though it had been sawn out, cast in concrete and shoved back in upside down. She had planned to have breakfast in bed: a fine reward after all her hard work. Imagining the blue tray with yellow flowers and a paper, spread luxuriously across the sheets, dotted with crumbs and bright red dollops of jam, her hair loose. She had not been expecting to flop fully clothed onto the sofa at four a.m., or for Trevor to appear a measly three hours later. Just as she had not been expecting the headache she has now when she was lighting one cigarette off another, rolling her eyes when Helen complained of feeling tired, uncorking another bottle of rosé.

Well, I've certainly ballsed up my chances this time. Last night—she will soon write, but now, right now, she has to attend to Trevor.

She lets him in and watches as he does not wipe his shoes on the mat. Instead he storms forward to rattle a loose balustrade, stopping just before it comes free and leaving it to wobble where it stands. He is building a new wall, he tells her, along the front, so do not mind him when it is happening. As he speaks her eyes search the kitchen for something to assuage her headache. His stare greedily at the bare point of her freckled shoulder, where her jumper has sagged down.

'That'll be it then, I'll let myself out. You know where I am if you need me.'

When he slams the door the balustrade falls to the floor.

Safely restored back to her bedroom, where she'd hoped to wake up, Donna empties a sachet of aspirin into a glass of water and watches it fizz, nestling further down into the pile of pillows propping her up against the corner of the wall. Then she takes her pen and carefully runs back over the words *really darlings*, *absolutelys* and *aren't those interestings* for added effect, before continuing to write on the piece of paper laid out flat on a book against her knee. She is writing a letter, and the letter is for Susan Bloom; the little girl who'd play shop on rainy lunchtimes and whose adjoining garden wall was just low enough to share secrets over if you stood on your toes. She's known Susan for as long as she's known her own name. When her mother had been pregnant Mr and Mrs Bloom had moved in next door and, to her mother's delight, Mrs Bloom was pregnant too. Born just three weeks apart to women who'd shared the fears and excitements of their firstborn, and with no siblings to follow on either side of the fence, she and Susan felt more like sisters than friends. Growing up, that's what they'd told people they were; protesting violently whenever anyone pointed out Susan's olive skin and dark curls versus her own pin-straight hair and freckles. Although, since entering their twenties, what used to feel so firmly like the truth had found itself gently misshapen. The trial of being a teenage girl, which takes something different from everyone it puts to the stand, had produced at its end two decidedly different women.

While Donna had gone off to pursue ceramics in North Staffordshire, Susan remained living in Basford, where they were born, working as a teller for the Halifax bank. Susan was proud of the job, which she deemed to be a little more sophisticated than the Co-op where Sally Ward had ended up, or the schoolwear shop that had claimed Julia Shaw. And she liked, she was pleased to discover, numbers. She liked the endless processes you could subject them to with the knowledge that they would all come out intact at the end. It calmed her, to know that all life's mysteries were only ever a miscounting. Mystery was not easily welcomed by Susan. Every night, as she floated towards sleep, she would fight it – beginning with the crowd of neon spots, faces, unformed thoughts and ragged light, crowding in on top of the day's memories. From the centre of her still body she'd draw the silence in, slowly smoothing the chaos out into a great expanse of untouched snow, ready for another day.

Since the age of twelve Susan had kept the bottom drawer of her bedroom dresser filled with tea towels and chair backs, collected from second-hand shops and hand-embroidered, with unquestioning pride in the home economics class of her secondary modern. In moments of panic or uncertainty she would open this drawer and caress her accumulating wares, soothing them like her mind at night. The cause of the panic, more often than not, was that these items would never find a use, threatened as they were by the neon chaos of her dreams; but now, to her unadulterated joy, they would not go to waste. In June she will marry Paul Baddeley and her bridesmaids will be dressed in the deep-sleep calm of baby blue. She will also, unwittingly, enter a life that Donna privately deems a disappointment.

Not that it mattered. Each letter between them shared a purpose entirely independent of its reply; like jelly being poured into a mould, their personalities set sweetly in their obverse, defined by what they were not.

What went so wrong last night, I hear you ask? Well. Rose, in one of her boisterous moods, started showing me off to Lizzie's tres importante guest. I know she meant well, and I should be pleased, but between you and me I could have died a death. She just kept pushing me on him at Belinda's, saying what a talent I am yadda, yadda, yadda, and of course I was mortified! I can't bear to be the centre of attention like that. I go bright red immediately and have to retreat, and yet, I crave it – it's what I daydream about all day long! I don't know.

It's all very well getting all religious in the workshop, but then you have to trot them out and watch people decide whether they want to own them or not, which throws me every time. Why I constantly subject myself to these ritual assassinations I'll never know. This morning I woke up full of thoughts like surely my time would be better spent feeding the starving masses or digging the roads?!

You'll be pleased to hear, however, that I sold the lot, so I won't need a shovel just yet!

But seriously, I got in such a tizzy about it. I simply hate being put on the spot like that, which is where the hangover comes in of course. I suppose I should get up and back into the workshop to make a start on the new batch now the shelves are empty, but I feel too bad. Honestly, someone should bat me about the head! I've got so little time for the workshop as it is now the cafe has started opening for dinner, and there I go getting shitfaced and slowing myself down. But you see I have to slow myself down like this, otherwise I just run about like a headless chicken. See the problem?

3

Nicola Long, sitting at a dimly lit desk in the Feminist Assembly reading room, could precisely see the problem. She rubbed her eyes, which had been close to closing, letting them readjust to the fuzzy lemonade light. Particles of dust raged pointlessly in front of her. The word 'tizzy' jangling around inside her head.

This was exactly how *she* felt. The thrill pulled a thread across her chest; Nicola wasn't just overhearing, she was being overheard! She lifted her head above the dust but the two other women reading in the Feminist Assembly remained bent and hushed, unaware of and unmoved by her discovery.

4

I can't even remember putting my keys in the door. I've thrown up twice since Trevor left and have been completely incapacitated since. Sometimes I think it isn't worth the effort! I'm perfectly happy making pots in private, so why do I feel like whenever something like this happens I have to be the most impressive person in the room? The work should speak for itself. Except it never does. Of course, the only ones that get on in this world I've noticed are those that have perfected speaking in its place. Cult of personality and all that, like John and his Jesus in blue jeans performance, throwing on a kick-wheel and singing about Zen Buddhism. I, on the other hand, am all form and no philosophy, and I live in fear of being outed as a fraud! It's days like this I wonder if I shouldn't just give it all up. Would you still write to me if I packed it all in to go and live in the wilderness?

Outside, the rain picks up again. Pattering against the window to the pace of Donna's fluttering eyelids as her pen rolls to the floor. Swaddled in a patchwork quilt of pale pinks and mismatched octagons of paisley, she falls asleep with the pages on her chest. Hands sinking into mud. She dreams of her pots as if they were people. Back in the workshop, they speak to her in quiet voices, squeaking with doubt as she tries to retrieve them from the kiln. Unpacking it alone at night she has taken to tying a brick to each foot to stop herself from toppling in, as someone suggested she might. Bending her waist over the edge and reaching down with her hands, like a pearl diver slipping off a boat into the ocean. But the pots resist. You were wrong, they say, as she tugs at them with arms outstretched, unable to coax them out and into the parade. We're not perfect. We're no good. Useless. Crap!

Maybe if you had company, she thinks, so she undoes her ankle tethers and dives in with them. The weight makes the floor give way. It falls through with a terrible crash. Shards flying, the ocean in flames.

I wonder if I shouldn't just give it all up, copied out in pencil by Nicola Long.

The Feminist Assembly was a small, underfunded archive dedicated to women's art in Poseidon House, an ailing purpose-built office block on Southwark Street in London. Flaking concrete framed the 1950s green lettering of the building's name above tired, heavy glass doors. In the foyer a series of signs met visitors beside a cold stairwell. One stated that the lift was out of order. Another, in bright logoed plastic, designated the top two floors as belonging to the artists' co-operative that was currently letting them out as studio space. A sign for the vaguely named Yeti Ltd had slipped down inside its smashed glass frame. The floor beneath, with its dislodged ceiling panels, abandoned extension cords and pilled gravel carpets, lay unclaimed and the remaining floor, the building's first, was marked by a screen-printed poster, pushed into the drywall with pins. The poster showed a butterfly, its body a human forearm with a clenched fist, its wings crammed with lettering, barely legible:

The Feminist Assembly   Archives and Reading Rooms.

First left up the stairs – ring bell for entry! Scrawled in marker underneath.

The reading room windows faced directly onto Southwark Street, still low enough to be level with a bus's top deck. In an attempt to preserve a little sanctity, Marcella Goodwoman had covered them with posters, screen-printed like the one in the foyer. On thin paper in varying shades of pink, they carried block capital slogans in black ink: MALE ARTOCRACY IS IMPOTENT! and COME OUT! they commanded of traffic in standstill. The posters filled every inch of the glass, giving the Feminist Assembly's light an overwhelmingly warm hue, as if the sun were forever either rising or setting. To Nicola Long, who'd been visiting the archive regularly for the past couple of weeks, this sealed the place off like a vacuum. It reminded her of sitting on the hem of a parachute in the hall at work, rushing in to be enclosed by a puffed cocoon of silk. The only part of her job she liked.

When Nicola wasn't at the Feminist Assembly, she worked as a nursery nurse at a primary school in Zone Three. She spent her time there wiping yellow Frubes off the faces of children and asking them what colour their feelings were, holding out a laminated rainbow for them to point to. In her lunch breaks she'd lie on the floor of the disabled toilet with the door locked, staring at the ceiling and thinking about how she'd got there; the small windowless room having been deemed preferable to the staff room, where, over strong tea and turmeric-stained tupperware, her colleagues spoke with their dignity angled away from her. After closing the toilet lid in a minor act of self-preservation she would stretch herself out on the orange linoleum, whose gritty, palliative texture was swirled from up close with flecks of silver. At five-minute intervals an air freshener on a timer sprayed the caustic scent of apricots into the room. Four lame sputters made the total of her break.

After finishing at the nursery she made the long bus journey back to her flat, her voice and feet aching from what she did not care to do. Nicola Long did not want to be a nursery nurse. She wanted to be an artist. Being an artist was the reason she'd chosen the job, which finished at three p.m. The spacious afternoons this left her with were where she would make that happen. When she'd graduated from her bachelor's degree in sculpture, she and two friends had scoured the Internet to find the shabbily converted studios of a disused warehouse, formerly used for burning waste, and every weekday at three-fifteen she had raced there. The atmosphere in those formerly hot rooms was urgent and optimistic. All three had graduated to relative approbation and the desire to retain it kept their hands warm and working, making small, squashed forms from clay, fuelled by the furious energy of the innocent. Nicola would fill her shelves with shape after shape, each one more solid and hopeful than the last. Bubble-wrapped and ready. Waiting.

She had not been able to catch whatever it was she thought she'd seen coming towards her. Meetings with curators were fudgy and uncomfortable; gallery openings sank under the weight of warm beer, loose handshakes and forgotten names. No longer able to justify the cost of a studio, Nicola retreated to her bedroom where she attempted to keep the bubble-wrapped landscape, now stored under the bed, illuminated by the lighthouse of her phone; posting photographs of the objects she'd made to the Internet with the same fervour as she posted her face. But the praise was always as quick as it was impossible to hold. Compressed into numbers, then moved along by the date. The hearts swelled, and then they burst. Now, when she took the bus home from the nursery, the only burning desire she felt was for sleep. It held a handkerchief of chloroform to her mouth as the bus swayed past the cut-back trees, boarded-up windows and social housing, all being slowly bulldozed into the blank of a cheque.

There is nothing left here to imagine a future with, she would think as she watched the years pass by through the glass. Which is how she got to: *I wonder if I shouldn't just give it all up.* It was the thought she'd been having when she'd first seen the posters in the Feminist Assembly's windows, travelling home on the bus from Waterloo. Having never heard of the Feminist Assembly, she looked it up on her phone. For women, by women: the Assembly is a place for women to deposit unique documentation of their art and artworks, the website said.

Nicola had gone to Waterloo to get an abortion. Or more specifically, to take the medication that would induce one, at the sexual health centre on Burrell Street. Though they'd said on the phone she should have someone to take her home, she hadn't wanted that. She would manage on her own. She would manage on her own because she didn't want anyone to see how she knew she was going to behave. Her reaction had surprised even herself, and she didn't know how to explain why she was taking it so unexpectedly seriously. Why she felt like she was splitting down the middle, the way a watermelon might if you dropped it. Everyone else she knew had treated it as a minor inconvenience, if that.

'It's so easy,' Alice had said. As had Naomi and Fran and Jude. 'Honestly, it's nothing. You're basically in and out.' Which was true. She'd arrived, and when her turn came the nurse had taken her into a small room for questioning, before instructing her to take four pills. Two on her tongue, two pushed up inside of her. Then she was out. But it had not been nothing.

Nicola made the journey from the clinic to her flat in the time she'd predicted it would take; some hours before the contractions started. She hadn't needed anyone with her and she was glad. When the pain finally started, she cried like she had not cried since she was very, very small: in loud, ugly, open-mouthed heaves. It's the hormones, she told herself, trying to rationalise her behaviour. *Tomorrow you will feel just as you always did.*

On her eleventh birthday Nicola had been given a film camera by her parents. It was silver and compact with round edges. The following month she had taken it on a family holiday to Berwick-upon-Tweed, wearing it proudly around her neck on a purple beaded strap for the entirety of the trip. Two weeks after their return home her father stood in the doorway of her bedroom, filling its frame with his outraged bearing. He held in his hand a shiny plastic envelope full of just-developed photographs.

'They're all of the floor,' he said. 'I will not pay for you to get your photographs developed if you only take photos of the floor.'

Nicola raised her head from the book she had been reading and asked to see. It was nothing but sand and grass and open water. The crimps the tide made on the beach.

'This one is of the sky,' she offered.

'That is not the point, Nicola Long, and you know it. It costs a lot of money to get film developed. In future, if you can't use something properly, you won't get to use it at all.'

Nicola had no plans for a family just yet, and though she was very fond of her boyfriend Ben Gibbs, with his Mies van der Rohe coffee-table books and his small, sweet-natured dog, he did not strike her as The Father. She wasn't crying because she wanted to keep the baby. She was crying because no one had asked her if she would.

After the cramps had subsided, lying with her laptop on her chest, Nicola remembered the Feminist Assembly's rosy wall of affirmations and the description on its website.

A place for women to deposit, it had said. The fish swam into the net. She emailed to make an appointment.

5

Donna hangs her favourite blue dress out to dry in the first proper sun they've had that year. While the silk is shaking itself free of water in the breeze she leans her head over the side of the bathtub and washes her hair on her hands and knees. Wrapping it in a towel, she returns to the garden to find Helen and Rose lying on the grass, humming an unidentifiable song. Their feet are dirty and their dresses are pushed up over their heads, making the tune strange and muffled. Their stomachs, already burnt, are bright red.

'What *do* you look like?'

'Well we didn't want our *visages* to burn,' says Rose through the fabric covering her face, 'and anyway you *have* to burn first. You need a base tan.' As she speaks she rolls over, presenting her naked behind, imprinted with strands of grass, to the sun.

'What time is dinner?'

'Kevin said six.'

Helen rolls over now too.

'Kevin?'

'Yes, Kevin.'

Helen loves Kevin. God knows why. He looks like a trout if you ask me but hey ho, each to their own. Anyway, because of this thrilling development we now have to do everything as a six. She thinks that because Rose and Simon and my Patrick and him are all friends that if she tags along he might get tricked into thinking it's some kind of triple date scenario and just go along with it and couple up too? I mean, good luck to her. He seems dim enough to fall for it, she might as well try. Anyway my flower, I've just been presented with a rather large glass of champagne perry and I wouldn't want to be caught drunk in charge of a biro. I'll tell all tomorrow . . . I will write the rest on the other side of the page so if you're feeling in need of some amusement you can place a bet. Will Helen or won't Helen succeed in seducing the illustrious Kevin?

It seems I am the bearer of bad news. No joy for our Helen I'm not-so-sad to say. Although I have to admit it's partly my fault. No, I didn't say anything. But I did get us all off our faces. First, the six of us went to the Taj Mahal. I had vegetable curry and it was delicious. When we left it was still light out which seemed almost like a miracle, it's been so grim for so long, so of course I suggested we all make good use of it and go to the park for a smoke. The first Spring of the decade! We had lots of very high-minded conversations about what we think the 1980s will be like which all dissolved the minute we had to try and get home. You know the hole in the floor of the old Mini? Well it's now so big you can see the ground through it. I mean it: you can actually see all the tar and squashed birds whizzing by beneath you as you drive. As you can imagine, in our newly altered states this seemed hilarious. We had to pull over God knows how many times because we were all giggling so much. In the end Helen and I had to drive home with me doing the steering and her doing the pedals because neither of us had the faculties to do both! We only took a small wedge out of Trevor's new front wall for the trouble.

Anyway, the main point of this letter is not to tell you about my zombied antics but to ask your very reliable and grown-up opinion on something. I think Patrick has been hinting at moving in together. I don't want to get ahead of myself but I feel very torn about it. On the one hand I love having my freedom, but on

Nicola turned the page.

She did not, at least not anymore, write letters and post them to an addressee. To her, the practice existed only as an exercise in whimsy: hiding messages in envelopes a quaint way to assure privacy, like veiling a bride. Sometimes Nicola was enlisted into lengthy email exchanges to pick over the bones of a break-up or to assess why a friendship might have fallen apart, which as a teenager she'd felt compelled to print out and keep in a box beneath her bed, but it hadn't occurred to her to retain a paper copy of anything so personal since. All the conversations that constituted her life existed in a hurricane of data which even she didn't consider worthy of requesting, as was her right. The nearest she'd stretch to was a screenshot, sometimes, for 'proof'.

The last letter she remembered writing that hadn't taken the shape of a postcard was when she was a child. Despite living within walking distance, Nicola and her schoolfriend Katie Edmond had kept up a written correspondence. They had both recently read *I Capture the Castle* and believed their inner monologues to be filled with intrigue of literary worth. For added entertainment, they would decorate the envelopes in novel ways. Once Katie wrote Nicola's address in the form of a crossword. When it arrived she could see the postman had filled it out, his good-humoured block capital letters all in place. Across: comes after one, three letters. This had thrilled Nicola, but it had filled her with envy more. She knew she wouldn't be able to think of anything so inventive in response and she resented the challenge it posed. Shamed by her lack of imagination, she declared the game childish, and it stopped.

Reading, on the other hand, was easy. All she had to do was sit very still and the world would shift; inviting her in as a citizen, liking a tweet because it was true enough she *could* have written it. Watching, Nicola soon learnt, was also a form of taking part. A form that, sitting at her quiet desk in the Feminist Assembly, she felt impossible to get wrong.

That evening, travelling home from the archive, she watched the story of a party that had taken place the previous night. Its gloss, as far off and odourless as the afterlife, now hers to hold. She pressed her temple against the bus window and arched her body over her phone. Small white chicken bones rolled around her feet. The passenger next

34

to her lifted a papery ankle to scratch before lowering it down with a cough. Nicola held her breath and hunched some more. From the centre of her palm girls she sort of knew with rosy cheeks, long white whiskers and candy pointed ears posed in a bathroom mirror before disappearing. She tapped the left-hand side of the image to play the scene again, focusing this time on the face of one girl in particular, making bored, blank criticisms. Nicola's eyes narrowed, she bent her head forward. Pawing at the screen, she played the scene again, again, again. Forcing time to tailor itself to her in a neat, looped, stitch.

6

The wind is disturbing the window frames, and Donna would rather bang her head against the wall than choose an outfit. She paces back and forth until Patrick declares the situation to be far from the end of the world and abruptly leaves the room, making it feel as though her head had been banged for her. To steady herself after what she will later call a fight she places her hands flat, facing in opposite directions, on the Formica surrounding the sink. In front of the mirror she makes her shoulders rigid. The unventilated air of the bed and breakfast's small bathroom is sodden with pink soap. She can't name what it is that's putting her on edge, but the heart of it ran close to various scenes she couldn't shake. Scenes that made her feel like a fraud; the broken lightbulb in the kitchen, the musty smell that followed her from the cafe where she worked washing dishes, the damp stain growing above her bed.

Something very close to dread, Susan.

The event for which she cannot ready herself is a small show of her pots in a town she doesn't know. She takes a few more breaths in front of the mirror and then returns to the bedroom. Patrick has left. From the window she can make out the smoking spectre of his silhouette on the street below, marching up and down the pavement in either anger or impatience. For a brief moment she imagines it as a kind of surrogate anxiety on her behalf and is touched, but she is old enough to know wishful thinking when it pricks and so, jolted by the sight of the waiting man she accepts what she has on and leaves the room. They walk in silence across the wet paving stones towards the taxi rank.

As they drive the image of the mould at Bambury Avenue pools gently inside her. Ash from a cigarette has marked her cheesecloth skirt. She thinks of how as a very young child everyone had believed that the poorest children at school were contagious. People had not wanted to touch them. If they sat on a chair, that chair was spoiled. She thinks of her pots on show and wonders how strongly they smell of an ineffable need.

Nicola tapped her knuckles on the glass panel in the middle of Marcella's office door.

'I'm leaving early today.'

'That's fine, sweetheart, just remember to sign out. Anywhere interesting?'

'Only the pub.'

In the draughty toilet block of Poseidon House, Nicola put the tote bag she carried around with her on the window ledge above the hand dryers. From it she took a stub of lipstick and a can of dry shampoo. Using each to the best of her abilities, she smudged some colour on her cheeks and attempted to unify the strands of her fringe. Then she re-tied the laces on her tattered black boots, a pair similar to ones described by the potter in an earlier letter and which, on reading, had sent a bolt of recognition straight to her heart. In the sink she washed her hands, trying to remove the morning's traces of felt tip and PVA glue. With her nails she scratched at where the glue had caught on the hairs above her wrist. Before leaving the mirror she made a series of faces, turning this way and that. She searched for something in her image the same way she'd watched the sky during the picnic she and Lyn, Miss Heal to the children, had staged that morning. Anxiously checking the movements of the clouds and trying to gauge their thickness, hoping they'd permit the ray of sunshine that would dignify their efforts. Every now and then, the glimmer of possibility. Nicola had felt warmth on the back of her neck with pleasure before it turned into the hot child-breath of Bobby Macintosh, whispering in her ear, red with shame and knocking his knees together. His small bottom stuck out and wriggling.

At the pub she handed Jason, whose birthday they were celebrating, a bunch of pink carnations she'd bought on the way.

'They're a nice shade, aren't they?' she said as if to verify, kissing him on the cheek and taking a seat at his side. Then she asked how he'd spent his day.

'Adrian bought me breakfast in bed and tut tut it hasn't stopped since then,' he said, raising a glass in demonstration.

'And you? What have you been doing?' Nicola told him she'd been at the Feminist Assembly doing research. She didn't mention cleaning up Bobby Macintosh's soiled tracksuit bottoms, or lying on the toilet floor. 'It's an archive,' she explained, 'for women artists.'

'Never heard of it.'

'Oh?' Raising her voice, 'Haven't I told you? I've found these letters, written by a ceramicist, a potter, in the seventies and eighties. It's uncanny, actually, how much we have in common, we—'

'I didn't know you were still making ceramics?'

Before Nicola could answer, more guests arrived and she was forced from her spot beside the birthday boy to let them through. Shuffling along the faded banquette she felt irritated by the exchange. True, she hadn't made any ceramics for some time, but that was not the point. They did have so much in common. It was a fact that had been making its claim on her, clear and immovable, for some time. She just hadn't had time to explain to Jason exactly why, catching his interest sufficiently. Maybe next time someone asks why she spends all her time in an archive no one seems to have heard of she should refine her reasoning. Skip straight to the important part.

Something very close to dread, Susan.

7

The cabbage rose carpet is coming up at the sides and the surface is littered with cigarette butts and dried shavings of mud from the underside of men's boots. By the time the bathroom door has loudly swung itself shut behind Donna, she is already back inside his bedroom. His snoring is heavy so she knows she is safe. Under his breath she searches silently for her purse, socks, keys. She casts a final glance over his face just to make sure, then slides out the door, through the kitchen, down the stairs and out onto the street. Walking fast and with purpose until the recreation ground at the end of the road. Once on the directionless flat of the grass, where she'd woken up was anyone's guess.

She tries to play through what she can remember in her head, but it is hard because her head, like her chest, hurts. She can see every possible scenario as clear as cut glass, intersecting with a mathematical precision, each line as deliberate as the last. There's the version where she is bug-eyed, game and monstrous. There is the less athletic attempt, all gaping mouths and limp limbs before she is pitifully put to bed. And then there is the third version. She has no memory of anything past eleven p.m., when in the red smoke of The Bonny Prince he had slipped something in her drink, and she had slung it down with a smile.

She unlocks a small gate used to keep dogs and children from mixing and walks across the bark chips to a swing, where she sits to catch her breath. The sun is rising over the houses and the air feels bleached with the wet scent of cut grass. Opening her blue clutch, she riffles about for a cigarette. The packet is crushed and empty but she manages to find a loose one, which she straightens and lights. As she smokes she examines the spotted mark on her forearm and wonders if it will bruise. *I suppose the only thing to be done about it is to forget it ever happened, which should be easy enough with my sieve for a brain.*

But someone had seen her leave his flat, its thin doorway squished between a Woolworths and the corner shop where everybody goes to buy their cigarettes, papers and milk. This someone had told a friend, who had told another friend, who eventually told the fiancée of the man she'd left snoring in bed. *The only real concern of the mob it would seem. Apparently she and him are engaged, or were, so now I'm social pariah number one and have been called a tramp down the grapevine more times since Saturday than I would care to tell you.*

I wish I was sensible like you. You would never land yourself in a ditch like this. Sensible Susan. Well, you don't know how lucky you are!

She stubs her cigarette out on the metal chain of the swings and gets up, making her way back out onto the grass. As she walks she notices that the crack in her boot has grown into a sizable tear. *Fucking typical. There must be something else that has gone wrong to tell you about while I'm here? Oh, yes. The car has another hole, this time in the petrol tank.*

On and on, round and round, la di da. What next I wonder? Where will the next pile of shit be coming from?

Susan Baddeley, née Bloom, stops reading and walks into her kitchen. She takes her plastic scales and a Pyrex dish out from the bottom kitchen drawer, checks the dial, then twists the small black knob at the back to return the weight to zero. Carefully, she weighs out a mix of currants, preserved cherries and dried prunes. They fall into a dark gummy mound. The small red pointer on the face of the dial wobbles underneath at a few ounces over what she wants, so she removes one cherry and then another until it twitches back to where it should be. Then she takes the tray and pours the fruit into the Pyrex dish, using her hand to make the mound level. The brandy is next. Moving aside the crystal glasses she was given as a wedding present, she reaches for it from the back of the drinks cabinet in the living room. The glasses are covered in a light and sticky dust so she carries them too, a finger in each one to lift the four at once, and places them in the sink as she passes to later wash and polish. The brandy goes over the fruit, poured on steadily until each piece is submerged. She leans forward a little to inhale its familiar pinch: Christmas.

Susan likes to make the Christmas cake in the first week of November so that it has time to mature and moisten, topped up every weekend with a glug of alcohol to keep it going. It's what her mother always did, and what, now that she's pregnant, she will do too. The fruit was always the most important part. The last thing to go in the bowl, they would make a wish as they stirred it in, big hands on small to guide the spoon. Health and happiness, health and happiness, health and happiness. The only undisputed wants. Her life thus far, proof of the preserves' efficiency. Here she was: healthy and happy, growing a person and baking a cake. *You don't know how lucky you are!*

So why did that feel like stepping on a pin?

We've all seen it but you, is what she read between the lines.

To the only child in the cinema who covered their eyes when the shark came, missing the arms in the air, the spurt of red, the deflated yellow lilo on the shore.

'What happened? Tell me!'

Everyone saw it but you, dummy.

She thought of the Thomas Hardy novels she'd exhausted as a girl with her heart between her teeth, surrounded by long grass, fog and driving rain. The things that came to her at night with their heavy sense of predetermination, flashing in a naked strobe of light.

She had so far evaded it. But nevertheless, she always kept one ear alert to the sound of tyres, footsteps, forced doors and cracked windows. Waiting. She envied her friend who she knew, now, would recognise the silhouette behind the glass. Better, far better, Susan thought, to know who's out there. To open the door and let him in, lie down and absorb the shock of it like a rubber mat under metal.

Does she wish for it? Stirring the fruit.

No, of course not. Of course she doesn't want that, would never. She knows these thoughts are strange, unwelcome, bad. Knows—

8

Before she can begin, the clay must be wedged. To wedge clay is to systematically slice it and slam it so that it is limber. It is hard work, and her body sways rhythmically back and forth, pushing with both hands, but she does not tire. This is because the kneading comes not from the muscles in her arms but from the weight of her body, and she uses the weight of her body correctly. When she feels she is done she presses her thumb into the surface, to see if it leaves an imprint; the clay suckers to the shape of its minute ridges with perfect immediacy. She frowns.

The purity of the material was beginning to trouble her.

No longer congruent with her view of the world, the feeling of pride she'd first felt was beginning to shift into dissatisfaction. She wanted the forms she made to seem as if they had grown up from the earth themselves, dragging everything under it up with them. She wanted them to have the mud-speed: the vibrating personality of matter in turmoil. Not as perfect as an egg, but as vivid as a land-slide. But, of course, once you fire something it's fixed. Often she would open the kiln to find that what earlier in her hands had wriggled with a kind of luminescent truth, *on and on, round and round,* now had the rooted face of an urn.

This one though, will do what she wants. She is determined. She places the lump in the middle of a sturdy wooden table and beats into it with her fist. Leaving at its end a base, she works into the hollow which reaches up around her wrist. When the thickness of the base feels about right she leans sideways with her elbows pointing out to form a bow and begins with her whole body a dragging movement. Starting with the tips of her fingers and carried through the momentum of her twisting shoulders she persuades the lump of clay towards the sky, all the while walking around it backwards. This action is repeated as the walls get higher and thinner. Moving swiftly, she begins to add short thick coils into and against the lump, moving back and forth at pace as if in a dance, reversing occasionally on the balls of her feet to avoid giddiness, circling the maypoles of her youth.

Donna stands back with her hands on her hips to look at what she has done. It needs disrupting some more. She fetches a handful of porcelain from the dustbin, where she keeps it wrapped in plastic, and pushes penny-sized lumps of it into the stoneware around the rim; the porcelain will fire at a different temperature to the stoneware, tearing at its sides in scorched open mouths of white. It will not be functional, this pot, not anymore. It will be better. It will look like it has suffered and endured.

Then she very nearly drops it. As she carries it to the drying shelf the cries of a baby fill the room, breaking what

46

was otherwise silence and making her jump. After taking a quick breath to steady herself she turns to the basket balanced on a high bench at her side, and coos.

'Don't worry, don't worry, Peg. I'll only be gone for a second.'

But she does worry. She worries about the dust in the air, or worse, that she will stick out an elbow to smooth a join and knock the basket off its perch, sending baby Peggy to the floor. It has happened before.

Helen, who Peggy belongs to, *has gone to Hebden Bridge for the weekend with Kevin, leaving me in charge again. Unnervingly, there have been an increasing number of babies in the workshop of late and I must say this has really forced me to reassess my plans – what I want. Not a child, obviously, but a workshop. A room of one's own, as it were. Crucially one sans nappies. It's what everyone wants, really. The sharing is only a jumping off point and always would be, but it seems this far off dream of independence has decided to reassert itself with a new urgency!*

Living through another winter at Bambury has been thankless, unhelped might I add by the addition of Peggy and Kevin in December. The conditions in our creaking old house, which occasionally does sparkle with the promise of alternative values and communal spirit and which I have to admit is almost enough, are on the whole unliveable. You would just die to see it, my flower! The damp has gotten so bad I can barely breathe at night and is cruelly responsible for the development of a nasty cough in all, including the smallest. Black mould everywhere. The worst has made its home around my headboard!

I was just about on the edge of an abyss what with the Mini being scrapped and the damp and well just everything, when Paddy (who is now firmly just a friend, thank you) introduced me to a pal of his at The Dog. Dev, who has just moved down to Hanely from Leeds.

WELL SUSAN.

I was sold immediately! Tall, dark, sort of nervous but mysterious energy and lots of thick black curly hair. Honestly so handsome I could have thrown up. He's from India Susan, can you even imagine? Oh, and he has the sweetest snaggletooth you've ever seen! He works at the local theatre doing box office type stuff but he writes poetry and wants to do a masters degree in sociology at some point. Anyway, we got set up on a date and I told him all about my pots and about my RCA ambitions and he seemed genuinely interested, asking all sorts of questions with full eye contact, no less. Amidst all this eye contact a not insignificant amount of vino tinto was consumed which resulted in him coming back to Bambury and, well, I shall spare you the details but needless to say it has been a whirlwind ever since! And (dare I say it so soon but I feel I have to before you can write back and do your usual naysaying) I think I am in love.

I feel very calm. Really ready for a change and some stability. No more drunken mishaps, no more ups and downs. Life has finally thrown me a rope and I am going to shimmy up it with all my strength!

Susan hears her friend's voice dancing in the air as she reads. Breathless and eye rolling, quick like heavy rain. Without thinking she rubs her baby bump, as if to calm what she carries from the pace. She sets the letter down beside a blue glass vase of chrysanthemums, where petals have fallen onto the kitchen table in a ring around the base. I should turn the heating down a notch, she thinks as she sweeps the petals into the palm of her hand, making a neat pile on the table's edge before carrying on.

She tries, this time, to imagine the voice differently: less frantic, more measured. More like her own. She tries at a little patience. A masters in sociology sounded to her like a reasonable life trajectory. Better than Patrick's, who as far as she knew sold stolen scrap metal. She reads the rest of the letter in Donna's newly invented voice, taking phrases like *on the edge of an abyss* with a heavy pinch of salt. She reaches the end with a feeling of lightness. Suppose they get married, she wonders, we could raise our children together if she did it soon.

Thank you for the book recommendation by the way. Your Anaïs Nin diaries look set to be right up my street. I'm only a few pages in but already hooked; the ultimate in neurotic self-absorption, like a kind of decadent St Teresa!

Lots of love,

Into a notebook Nicola Long copied out the words *decadent St Teresa* and underlined them twice.

9

'No,' said a little boy with his hands on his hips.

'Please,' pleaded Nicola, 'please listen.'

She laid her hands on top of his chubby fists in an attempt to soften the pose which alarmed her; it seemed too aggressive, too adult, for a child. For a long minute they stayed like that with their eyes locked before he squirmed out from under her and sank his tiny milk teeth into the flesh of her forearm. Flames of white. She exhaled slowly, resisting the urge to snap his fat little wrist clean in half. I shouldn't be here, I shouldn't be here, I shouldn't be here, she repeated to herself as the breath flowed from her lungs. She wanted so many other things.

She wanted to be an artist. She wanted to be prettier than she was. She wanted her friends to listen to her when she spoke, and she wanted, more than anything, to rest for a little bit. The boy ran off shouting HAHAHA.

Nicola closed her eyes. Inside them she held the image of green fields, wild poppies and butter-coloured lichen. When she opened them she looked at the clock and counted: five hours left. Catching her sitting with her eyes shut on a miniature chair, Bernie, a wiry cockney woman in her early sixties who'd taken it upon herself to wear a red pen on a lanyard around her neck, suggested she tidy the Home Corner.

'No,' thought Nicola.

Then, with her whole being she said it. Got up from her slumped position and walked past Bernie, right out the door. Outside the playground gates, heart beating, she texted her boyfriend Ben, who'd been telling her to quit for years. It was a pressing issue for him, and he had all kinds of schemes lined up for how she could better use her time: she could train as a hairdresser, for instance. All it would take was a few years in a salon to build up a clientele, and then she could go freelance. Be her own boss. Two jobs or so a day, with plenty of time left over to get a studio again: go there. Lily did it, he said, and she made a killing. Barely worked.

Fucking finally, was his reply. He wanted her to come to his office, where he worked as a software developer in a converted shoe factory on Regent's Canal, to have a celebratory pint in his lunch break. But Nicola was already marching in the wrong direction: towards the potter. *Her* potter, as she had come to think of her.

When she arrived at the Feminist Assembly, Marcella was sitting at her desk. The computer screen framing her silhouette in front was covered in post-it notes, so much so that to use it as it was intended would be extremely difficult, if not impossible. They crowded the black cube's sleeping face with reminders: Interrogating Archives meeting, 4 p.m. – get keys; slides for Elizabeth; Rosemary Spence Prize; abortion materials for Amy; biscuits.

'Just to keep the day-to-day ticking over,' Marcella had explained when Nicola asked about her irregular notice board. 'My long-term memory is fine, it's the short term that's the problem. But you know, it's never been a problem. Not ever! Because the real archive is in here,' and Marcella tapped her head. 'It's always been very fluid like that, very fluid, just so long as I keep the day-to-day ticking over.' As she said day-to-day for the second time she tapped a post-it note with 'tea bags!' written on it, just like she had tapped her head: dah-dah-dah.

'Early today,' she noted, before going to fetch the letters Nicola had come to read.

Once settled in her usual spot, she kicked off her boots under the desk.

Sliding down the riverbank she slipped through the clear green water to meet the potter underneath, now eight months into her fledgling romance and living in a *dear little cottage in Stone.*

The cottage had been Dev's idea. Throughout the spring of their romance his ideas had stepped forward as the shining star of their union. He had a lot of them. He held every conversation with two hands and ran with it; standing up to speak, getting on chairs to speak, smashing bottles against the wall to speak. He looked like no one else and he liked to be heard loud and clear. Walking up the drive, their first night in Bambury avenue, Dev had the idea to key Trevor's Cortina. Watching him scratch into the paintwork from above, Nicola thought of Ben, who'd never done anything remotely like that.

Donna had clapped in delight. Late into the night he would pour her glass after glass of whiskey while he talked and she listened, lighting one cigarette off the next as the capillaries in her cheeks burst quietly under the skin. But for all his theatrics, he had been brought up as nothing less than a prince, and his mother's son certainly wasn't going to marry a girl that lived in a quasi-commune engulfed in mould. So, Stone it was.

It's a small town, and has all the desirable qualities; town community, classy housewives, exclusive type fish shops, bakers, the list goes on. My bourgeois fantasies are thriving! You know, I was resisting the conventional life for so long, but now that it has presented itself to me quite naturally I must say it rather suits me. So it would seem we are not as different as you'd like to think, my dear.

I have quit the cafe once and for all. Dev makes, or seems to have anyway, enough for the pair of us if you add my dole cheques and occasional pot sale (undeclared of course) to the mix. I have taken to the unofficial role of housewife like a fish to water. It has given my days a lovely rhythm. I wake up to tea in bed, then usually take up some gentle task in the kitchen like doing the dishes or what have you, then I go off to my private workshop. Private workshop? I hear you ask. Well, in truth it is a shed at the bottom of the garden, but it's really coming along quite nicely. No kiln of my own I'm afraid but Roger (old college tutor, maybe you remember?) lives close by so I tootle all my bisque dry pots over to him in a wheelbarrow once a week. It's very peaceful here. Picturesque and very isolated. The only eyesore really is the landlord digging an atom shelter in the next field over. Actually, it is bliss. I know this to be true because I can read your letters without feeling mad with jealousy of your stable mind. In fact, you'd be knocked down by how normal I've been of late. I can't even remember the last time I was upside down drunk which would seem to be a record. Dev is quite into psychedelics at the minute, so all my excursions behind the eyes have been much more insightful and mellow.

One such insight is that I have decided to embrace the slowness of Stone with open arms. Let the career take care of itself for a bit. Having some space has made me think that if I manage to keep the pace up and my head down I might even have enough new work for a portfolio, that way I could finally try for the Royal College. I am looking at this chapter as a time of personal development and respite. We are going to get a dog and possibly some chickens. I am very happy, in case I hadn't made that clear.

10

How long had it been?

Since October. Since October, when Nicola had seen the posters in the window and looked at her phone and it had described what it was and she had gone. Now it was February, and she was standing outside a house in Mile End waiting to be let in. When Nicola decided Ben's hairdressing project was too much effort, her friend Alice had suggested Better Connections, an agency that procured 'young creatives' to teach art to troubled teenagers – or 'school refusers', as the agency called them. The hours were significantly shorter than at the nursery, never managing to stretch to after lunch, which meant that Nicola could spend every afternoon in its entirety at the Feminist Assembly, reading. She was pleased with the job.

The first student she had been assigned was a fifteen-year old girl called Francesca Russo, whose house she went to every morning for however long Francesca could be persuaded to sit down. Her task was to help Francesca with her art and design GCSE. Nicola could remember enjoying it when she had done it, but now, in its repetition, it struck her as almost unspeakably dull. The criteria for passing, as far as she could gather, seemed only to require research into famous artists and cursory attempts to mimic their artwork, making said research apparent. All of which had to be annotated in neat handwriting along pencil-drawn lines. Both Nicola and Francesca shared a desire to do as little as possible for as long as possible; Nicola because she was paid by the hour and Francesca because, well, 'refuser'.

Nicola watched as Francesca wrote the words TRACEY EMIN in a slow, careful bubble font, meticulously shaded in several hues of purple pencil crayon. Her wrist and arm were astoundingly thin. When Nicola had been vetted for work by the agency they'd told her about this, what they referred to as Francesca's 'condition'. Do not allude to it in any way, they warned. Treat her like anyone else, like someone whose upper lip does not show the outline of individual teeth. Nicola tried. She thought about it constantly, though, for how could she not? Nicola thought about this very young person as someone she believed to have gained an edge. She would watch the turquoise veins on Francesca's breastbone move as she added a glint of silver gel pen patiently to each letter, with a feeling that could only be described as jealousy; her frail body having accreted an aura of suffering like a halo.

Nicola was desperate for such a hat. Instead, she squatted somewhere much more mundane; updating her Instagram as regularly as possible with fevered attempts to prove her face was one like any other; grinning over and over again into the grid like a squirrel storing nuts for the winter.

When she watched Francesa, Nicola found her own efforts grotesque.

Each of Francesa's lessons were carried out in her kitchen on a small table in front of the fridge. The fridge was covered in magnets with phrases like 'A friend is a sister you chose'; 'I love to cook with wine, sometimes I even put it in the food'; and 'Growing old is not for sissies', emblazoned over the image of an elderly woman in a swimsuit stepping out from an icy lake. The first time Nicola noticed the old woman on the fridge, she'd felt a shadow rise in her throat.

11

We haven't found a bed yet so we sleep amidst a pile of pillows and blankets on the floor upstairs, like two children pretending to have found Antarctica. For the kitchen we have cobbled together a passable dining table and four stools from the scraps of wood and broken furniture lying about the atom shelter's construction site. Dev has managed to scrounge a telly and his grandmother conveniently passed, leaving us a sofa, a fridge and two armchairs.

In our rustic haven we have taken up a few wholesome pastimes such as gardening, i.e. finding and drying magic mushrooms, and making country produce, i.e. brewing dandelion beer and gorse wine by the bucketful. In between all of which a little decorating gets done. It's still a bit bare and unfinished but moving along at an OK pace given what a shell it was.

Of all the rooms, the conservatory is my favourite. The light is always so brilliant, it is the perfect spot to sit and sketch so long as I wear a good jumper. I have painted the window frames yellow and made some nice simple pots which go along the edge to put the daffodil bulbs in. The *only annoyance really is that bees are always getting stuck in there. They hurry in all merry and humming when the door is open and then can't find their way back out again, dozy buggers. Dev has become obsessed with saving them. Apparently they're important. He puts sugar and water in saucers, first balanced on the daffodil pots, then on the steps down to the garden, then the path leading to the shed, and the flower beds after that. He watches them like a monk! So patient, bless him, moving and waiting, moving and waiting, until they have drunk enough to fly off again revived, in the right direction.*

What he does not do is bring the saucers back in. They collect amongst the flower beds trapping smaller, less significant bugs than bees.

The image of squirming hoverflies, fruit flies and blue-bottles, with their legs glued in place and their wings giving out, repeats on her in the night. She takes it as an omen: the extreme tenderness, and then the forgetting.

12

'You're better than the last girl they sent,' Francesca said as Nicola sat gazing aimlessly at the kitchen walls. 'She'd take my phone off me until we finished. She'd sit on it.'

'Really? What happened to her?'

'I had to kill her, obviously. She's buried in the garden.'

Involuntarily Nicola glanced out at the well-kept, wet grass, frowning in what she knew was an embarrassingly uncomfortable way.

'No, but she was fucking lame. Into rockabilly shit.'

'What's wrong with that?' asked Nicola, who had a penchant for polka dots, in her most casual voice.

'Nostalgia's a disease.'

Nicola told Ben this as she diced an onion later that evening.

'Maybe she has a point?'

'Oh? From the man who worships the Bauhaus.'

'Design, yes. Furniture. But I do think . . .' Ben paused. He'd been about to top up their wine, but he placed the bottle back down on the table so as to elaborate his point first. A sign he was about to say something important.

'You, for example. I don't see where any of this research' – he lifted his hands, which were now free, to draw scare quotes in the air – 'you claim to be conducting is going? If it's as fascinating as you say, you know there are grants you could be applying for? Residencies? I can guarantee you that when they knock that building down, and they will, that archive will dissolve. Then what?'

His voice had taken on the high, strained quality it had when he was talking to his dachshund. He lifted the wine bottle again and poured. Taking a long sip as if he'd earned it, he said: 'Lily Topher's doing a residency in Wexford. They have rolling applications, I can get her to send you the link. You should really be thinking about the *contemporary* angle. What's the end goal?'

'Lily the hairdresser?'

'Lily's an artist, she just *cuts* hair, we've been through this.'

Nicola's eyes were beginning to sting.

'I just think that if you had some of her chutzpah . . . You could learn a lot from her, you really could.'

'You don't think I have chutzpah?'

'I think that you're depressed, Nicola.'

He gave her a look, then, that made her heart feel very small inside her chest. 'These onions. I have to wash my face,' she said, padding blurrily down the hall.

In the brightly lit bathroom Nicola examined her face in the mirror. The eyes that stared back at her were soft, wet and rimmed with red. She leaned forward on the sink for a closer look, until her nose almost touched its image. Along the bridge, taut pale skin and tiny dashes of more broken red. But it was the eyes that held her attention, growing further into her face the longer she looked. In the abysmal centre of each one the reflection of the room with her in it sharpened and expanded, gaining definition.

There you are, she thought.

She was speaking to the Dead Woman inside her.

She'd seen her before, the Dead Woman, on YouTube, in the howling eyes of Lena Zavaroni – the soft-spoken Scottish singer who had demanded a lobotomy and later died from its complications at the age of thirty-five. Nicola had watched the video of Lena Zavaroni performing 'Going Nowhere' countless times, pressing the spiralised arrow over and over until its surging feeling swallowed her. The video showed the former child star, whose voice had always seemed too large for any person, with her hands held to her temples; her eyes an eerie shade of Parma violet and her pupils darting back and forth, as if fixed upon something awful and unstoppable only she could see. Her whole being the breaking apart of cold compacted ice, crashing into the ocean. In the video Lena Zavaroni wasn't singing, she was pleading.

And still they're asked to hold the world together
Make it happen, give it children
Who in turn are, turning on to, going nowhere

When the song ends she blinks several times and her jaw twitches, brought back to herself and the stage in what looks like disbelief at the cry she just let out. When the audience applauds she takes a sweet and self-conscious bow, smiling like a child.

When Nicola was a child she'd been hypersensitive to insults and slights, as if when being made someone had not woven the membrane of her skin tightly enough, or remembered to close it off. Words got in easily. When she looked back on her formative years they struck her as sodden; a big, red, chubby cheek onto which claims of being left out or picked on fell in heavy droplets. Nicola's a wimp, Nicola's a wimp, ringing out across the playground while twigs slapped at the back of her calves. It wasn't fair! *Some* people got to walk through life with their frailty enshrined behind a steel wall. The steel wall of the sublime – their trouble with living having gained an ethereal elegance. Untouchable! How she envied them. Her inability to cultivate a convincing aura of tragedy had constituted, for Nicola, one of the great unfairnesses of her life.

The house she'd grown up in had been built on the rallying cries of Life isn't fair, Grist to the mill, Pull your socks up, and, her mother's personal favourite, simply: Tough. Whereas the figures that populated Nicola's ideal image of herself were people like Lena Zavaroni, and now, thanks to Marcella Goodwoman, the potter. People to whom no one would ever dream of uttering the word Tough, a scene as unthinkable as telling Christ to simply get down from the cross.

Oh, to join those ranks! She could not think of anything more exalting. It was the reason she kept coming back to the archive, day after day, month after month: to look at the Dead Woman she believed to be inside herself. She could brush her hair and hold her hand. She could bend her neck forwards and stare.

Nicola returned to the kitchen and picked up her knife, using the wide blade to scoop the onions she had diced into the pan. She did this in silence. Stoically, she thought.

'Sorry, Nic. I just worry about you sometimes.'

It was working. He came up behind her then and put his hands around her shoulders. She leaned into the embrace, ignoring the small feeling in her heart and focusing on the part that made her feel special. It was very romantic to be someone people worried about. Nicola turned around and let Ben kiss her.

13

Driving up a steep hill in Stone, Rose Hayden turns to Donna and asks:

'*Can* you die of gout?'

Their noses are tilted upwards and the backs of their skulls are wedged into the headrests, facing the grave, which is what makes them think of it: the game. The game is called How Will We Die?

They decide that Rex will drink himself to death because he already, almost, has. Kevin will probably die of gout. Teeth showing, they recite his favourite food: ginger cake with butter and cheddar thickly stacked on top.

Rose takes her hands off the wheel to twist her long red hair into a bun which she then skewers in place with a freshly sharpened pencil. The sun makes a blister on the windscreen.

'I', she declares, returning her hands to steady their path after a pothole, 'will be hit by a car, tragically, and in full view of all my children, of which there will be many. And *you*, Donna Dreeman, will die in the shower, very young, in mysterious circumstances. People will write books trying to solve it.'

'How chic!'

14

Susan pushes the bits of metal apart with her fingers, trying to imagine what their former shape could have been. She wonders if it is a present that did not survive the journey, but there is only one, and it is not to her taste. She rolls the nugget of plastic, coated to look like a pearl, between her thumb and forefinger as she opens the letter it fell from.

What is it? I hear you ask. Evidence, Susan. That's what. I thought that if I simply told you, you would try to talk me out of it. Not that I think you wouldn't believe me, just that you might think it wasn't as bad as all that, or that we could get past it or move on or something, but I hope this will serve as sufficient proof that it is as bad as all that. Look! Look how cheap and gaudy it is. It demonstrates a dismal lack of imagination on Dev's part but then again I'm not sure why I'm surprised. For all his high ideals it would seem that he, like everyone else, prefers a woman who looks as daft as a brush.

I suppose I should start at the beginning. I found the delightful earring you are holding under the bed. First, I stamped on it. Then I was going to leave it on the kitchen table (that we built!) and get straight in the car to see you, my flower, leaving him to find it on his own and put two and two together. But alas, I am both a coward and a misery glutton, so instead I sat myself down and waited for him to get home from the pub. We talked until three; him all It meant nothing, I'm a fool and me all sweetness and sap going We all make mistakes, no one's perfect, I love you, I need you etc which lo and behold got more and more hysterical until I was banging my head against the wall screaming What can I do differently? Why aren't I enough? What's wrong with me? You know the script. My most demonic display of insecurity yet, probably unhelped by the seventeen glasses of scotch I poured myself before he got in from the various bottles he leaves about. Needless to say, any chance of salvaging the situation is dead and buried now that I've shed my skin and shown the sorry worm underneath. Thankfully, he must have been even more horrified than I was because he didn't stick around for the sun to rise. He said I could stay in the cottage for as long as I needed and so that is where you find me, queen of my abandoned castle, pen in hand.

She puts it down and lights a cigarette, inhaling deeply. The compact sound of paper burning fizzes against the watery lining of her skull. She lied.

Donna didn't get straight into the car, not because she is a misery glutton, but because she thinks that's what Susan is, or can be. The thought of lying on Susan's sturdy plum damask sofa, newly upholstered in the neat, terraced house she owns with Paul, while Susan stroked her hair and told her about the way Paul sometimes looked at women, turned her intestines to stone. If she had to be made into that kind of female, she didn't know how she'd ever get up. Susan, whom she loved so deeply and who could make her feel so trapped, as if their fates were inescapably bound by being women, unaltered by what a person did or did not do. This was not supposed to happen to *me* is what she had wanted to scream most of all when she'd been wriggling free of her skin. The life she was building for herself was going to be marked by difference. Now she was Susan. But she wasn't only Susan, she was her mother, her aunt Trish. She was Pam, Trevor's wife. She had always watched Pam with such pity, with her proud skirt suits, red almond nails and brassy hair, out of date in its style but diligently maintained all the same. Donna would note the way Trevor's Cortina would come and go in the evenings, or the way his eyes moved so freely between her mouth and her breasts whenever she tried to tell him about the window that wouldn't close, and all the time she hated Pam for it, not Trevor. To be made foolish like that? Who could bear it? She thought a lot of things about herself, but fool had not yet been one of them.

I have been staring at this godforsaken earring for so long, with all kinds of horrors raging through me. I even put it on in front of the mirror, so I probably have syphilis now to top it all off. I know who she is, you know. He said her name and I knew immediately. Drinks at The Star sometimes with

Carroll and that lot. We spoke once, briefly, waiting for the loo. No tits.

Anyway, this bloody thing cannot be in my vicinity any longer lest I gouge my eyes out with it, so I am packing it off to you.

Bon appétit!

Susan picks the broken earring back up, now imbued with a personality, a certain threatening posture, leaning sullenly against a hand dryer in a bandeau top. She doesn't want it either. She gets up from her chair and walks over to the bin.

Later that evening, after doing the dishes, she is reminded of its presence, lounging tartily on top of the eggshells. Looking up from the sink, she catches a glance of herself reflected in the window. Tall with wide shoulders. An ironing board, they used to call her. Bottle-rimmed glasses sit on her stubbed nose below a perm of thick dark hair. Something about the earring and its winking disfigurement was laughing not at Donna but at her. With one Marigold-clad hand she pushed it deep down into the waste.

15

In an effort to build up her portfolio, Donna has been working later and later into the night. Anything she makes that doesn't meet the mark she takes a hammer to. The results of these massacres have provided her with a well-defined path down the middle of the garden. It crunches underfoot as she walks back to the cottage, her way lit only by a bare lightbulb dangling beyond the kitchen window. Once inside she takes off her dusty jeans and threadbare t-shirt, leaving them on the doorstep, and walks naked through the house until she finds an old nightie slung on the back of a chair. She slips it over her head with her arms up, then pours herself a generous glass of warm white wine and lights a cigarette. Dropping ash as she walks, she hunts about for a pen, before setting herself down on a cushion in front of the Rayburn to write.

Single, alas, and with life out there waiting to dig its claws in. Am I sad about Dev? Yes and no. The truth is my life exists in a portal between two worlds, and men disrupt this.

~

She takes a long drag.

There is the world of clay, where everything is ruled by fire and force and where the images in my head get pushed out through my fists into something real. And then there is the other one: the soggy world of the mind. With Dev, the latter seemed to overtake everything else. I lost all conscience for work and would just sit about doing nothing, pulling apart split ends, watching *him. Wondering what he was thinking and how I could please him, and so, of course, the rot set in. I didn't speak to you like this before because I couldn't understand it, but now that he has gone I can see it. I can see how much my focus had lost its edge.*

It would seem my *lot in life is that I am too committed to the world of fire and force to share it with anyone else. It throws my sense of balance right off. I am glad he did what he did. I even think I might have been craving it. Why else would someone let something as small as an earring tear their whole person to bits? I see now how stupid it was to build my happiness around him, and how little space there was outside of that. You probably knew before I did that I was* only *playing at being an adult, playing at keeping house. It was never where I belonged. I do not want to be a housewife clattering about some dinky-do cottage. I want to go to the Royal College. I want to set up my own workshop (shed notwithstanding). I want independence. Recognition! I want to live!*

My struggle is a personal one involving my work and my individuality and is precisely the reason why I cannot have a relationship: if I am to stay intact I must make myself as solitary as possible. I have to accomplish at least some of what I want before I can rest in somebody else's arms. I seem to have gone through agonies of loneliness at night, pacing about, feeling scared of the dark and the fields, but now I say to myself: this is my night, my space. This is a minor breakthrough for me and it means I am finally able to enjoy my solitude.

16

She stood, grinning in black and white, no bigger than an index finger, stepping out of a lake somewhere very far north. Her chest puffed up like proofed dough. Trees at the water's edge lined her shoulders in a row of blown-out candle wicks. The flowers on her costume, made velvet by the wet. A swimming cap sat on her head like a big, polished knee. Over it, in an arch: Growing old is not for sissies.

'Got everything?' Francesca's mother, coming in from the garden with gloves on, asked the young woman in front of her fridge. Stepping out of a daydream to meet her, Nicola replied that she had, thank you.

'Do you want to take one of ours?' Pointing to a plastic umbrella stand in the shape of a cat and adding, 'It looks like it's going to start soon.'

Nicola raised a hand in mild protest.

'Suit yourself. See you Monday, sweetheart.'

Walking to the end of the Russos' street towards the bus stop, Nicola made up her mind never to go back. She had been visiting their house for just over a month and it was starting to make her feel nauseous; something about teenage girls, like slipping softly backwards. Expecting another step at the top of the stairs only to drop with a jolt when you raised your foot to meet it. There was the way Francesca spoke to her mother, with her narrow lips jutted out and her chin in her chest, flipping her mother the finger, furtively, and only for Nicola to see, as if they were in on it together.

'Bitch,' she would say when she left the room.

Not wanting to associate herself with a woman who kept umbrellas inside the plastic body of a cat, Nicola never said anything to the teenager that would indicate disapproval. Instead she just smiled blankly and continued watching the videos Francesca liked to show her. Today's video had starred Francesca lip-syncing to a low hum, portrait not landscape, and oddly timed, as if ever so imperceptibly sped up. Her hair, flicking like a live thing and her eyes blurred like sherbet sweets. Dropping down, down.

Being a teenage girl had always seemed to Nicola like some kind of esoteric angel cult, and she had tried, when it was her time, very hard to join it. She had bought magazines printed on thin, not quite glossy paper, with roll-on body glitter in plastic pouches attached to the covers. Inside, they told her fortune through horoscopes and flow charts. You are a shy person. You are a pear. All the images accompanying these predictions showed skinny, smiling child-women bouncing on beds in days-of-the-week underwear, beating each other lightly with pillows.

Stars. Puzzles. Cringes. Music. The feathers falling about their impossibly hairless limbs like dandelion dust in summer. She'd watched them bounce through the keyhole of her own body, already too awkward and immobile to imagine leaping with such abandon. Francesca, spinning inside a reel with downy cheeks, was still trying to break down the door. Nicola wanted to join her. She hated that she wanted to. Nostalgia was a disease.

'My head feels heavy,' said Francesca as they tidied away the crayons and coloured pens. 'Like there is a weight in it, and somebody is pushing down.' Disclosures of this kind were not uncommon. Compared to the tutor who'd sit on Francesca's phone, Nicola's absent-minded engagement had been mistaken for compassion, establishing her as the primary confidant for a girl with very few people to talk to.

'Does yours feel like that?' Francesca asked.

Despite the immediate halo her thinness had given her, Francesca, Nicola had since decided, did not belong to the sacred troupe of the sublime. Her outlook was callous and her fingernails were covered in coagulated glitter. Real martyrs had a lightness of touch. They planted daffodils. She thought of Ben who, at this very moment, was probably worrying about her as he had said he did. The idea made her feel light, too.

'My head feels fine,' Nicola replied, avoiding the jolt.

Nicola imagined the lightness she felt was probably not unlike being trepanned. Something she fantasised about often. Its pleasures struck her as obvious. Stopping just short of the dura mater, a drill bit, designed to cling onto what it has cut through like a corkscrew, would remove a small nub of the skull. The puncture it made in the skin would soon heal over like any other wound, but the skull, with its freshly made hole, was opened forever. No longer burdened by a forehead fused together, she might once again let the wonder in. The accounts Nicola had read on the internet described a cold, quick fizz when the circular fragment of bone was removed and the air rushed in. She could conjure what that would feel like without any imaginative effort, as natural as breathing. A kind of hissing from deep inside your brain as the cool air finally touched it. At last!

Whenever things were not going the way she wanted them to, she would press the knuckle of her index finger firmly into the middle of her brow and summon the longed-for sound, to her great relief, its applause filling her ears like Pop Rocks.

Tssssssssssssssssssssss. For that alone was joy.

Pulling her sleeve over the tops of her fingers, she made a smear on the steamed glass of the bus window, from which to look out from. It continued its graceless lumber past the low-hanging branches and peeling houses until the eventual flatline of a dual carriageway, where the sun presented itself from behind a Big Yellow Storage. Nicola untangled her headphones. She checked that the L and R were in the right place before pressing them into the corresponding ears and tapping her finger against the flat of glass on her thigh to resume the podcast she liked. From the polished parquet floor of his dingbat apartment on Santa Monica

Boulevard, the nasal voice of Mike Austindorf reached her through the wires. As always, he promised to elucidate the hidden formicary of meaning that surrounded her ennui like a mist. The veiny hands of his vocal cords turned over stones in Laurel Canyon to find CIA agents crouching beneath them. Marilyn Monroe, she learnt, was not a drug addict but a soothsayer.

'There's something special about me,' Marilyn said through Mike, who was squeezing his voice into a high and breathy impersonation, 'I'm the kind of girl they find dead in a hall bedroom with a bottle of sleeping pills in her hand.'

The words travelled through pylons and satellites to shine on the floor of the disabled toilet of the nursery where she used to lie, as if it were a bruise surfacing from somewhere deep inside; her humiliated sanctuary. On its floor, beating, was the tender kernel of her struggle. 'Nothing is an accident,' Mike Austindorf told the quivering animal he found there. Its velveteen ears prickled, eager for confirmation of what Nicola had suspected all along: there was something special about her too. Twenty minutes slipped into a turning and the potter she was travelling towards appeared. She sailed across Nicola's forehead, kneading clay free of air at a workbench. The logic of her movements marbleised with the American voice wading through her temporal bone. *On and on, round and round.*

Taking her phone from her lap Nicola drafted an email to Better Connections telling them she wanted to quit.

~

The letters sat waiting at her desk. She was there with such unwavering frequency that Marcella no longer bothered taking them back into the store each night.

To tell you the truth my love, I'm beginning to feel a bit ridiculous stuck out here on my own all day and night. I speak to no one and for so long that whenever I use my voice it comes out as a croak. Ribbit, I say to Roger when I go four doors down to use the kiln. My days are spent trudging up and down from shed to house, and it is so cold I have a perpetual headache from always screwing my jaw tight to stop from shivering. No money and no social life, it pains me to report. Only pots. And I must admit, I am starting to feel a bit scared in the cottage alone at night. I hear so many noises. What a baby I have become. And treated like one too! Now that I am alone no one thinks me capable of anything. All my married friends keep boo-hooing at me, saying now you'll have to be sensible and live a normal life like the rest of us *or* now she'll have to get a real job. *Even mum said as much.* Why don't you give it up, dear, *she cooed when I phoned her for the hundredth time in floods of tears,* You've *tried the artist thing,* she said, *now come home for a little while.*

Well I won't. I won't give them the satisfaction.

This has all been very illuminating to say the least. It proves that all along no one ever believed in me, only now that I am sans man they feel they have the authority to come out and say it! I mean God, have you ever felt you weren't a viable proposition?

~

Nicola's phone lit up. It showed a text from Alice, and the time of the Women in Clay dinner.

I could meet you at the station and we could walk there together, it said.

Nicola had not been invited. She was only aware the dinner was happening because of Alice, and she would be going as her guest. When she'd had a studio, Alice was who she'd shared it with. Now Alice had a much larger one, subsidised by a property developer whose logo was the shape of a crown.

Maybe, Nicola wrote back. Through the spyglass of her phone she had watched previous Women in Clay dinners, scrutinising the ease with which all the dressed and shining women softened into a mirage of linen shirts, gold earrings and shared resources.

'We're closing soon,' Marcella came over to remind her. 'You've got ten minutes. Evening plans?'

Nicola had been looking forward to going straight home, making a tuna salad and eating it in bed in front of the series she liked. The 'maybe' to Alice had only been polite, but something in Marcella's question carried an air of – what exactly? Sadness? Sympathy? Something far from confidence in any case. The lightness didn't feel so pleasant, then.

Have you ever felt you weren't a viable proposition?

'I'm going to an arts dinner, for women who work with clay.'
'Oh how interesting, like our potter. Is that what you do?'
'Yes.'

~

80

I can be at the station for 7, she texted Alice. Will you wait?

Alice was leaning against a brick wall beside the entrance to Holland Park station, wearing a navy slip dress and off-white snap cardigan, reading a book. Her hair was neatly weighted in two calm plaits. When Nicola saw her she shrank. Her skirt had insisted on twisting backwards as she walked the long passages of the London underground and tugging it constantly into place had bullied her journey, drawing up a faint sweat. She regretted her decision to come; the dinner, where everyone would look just as lovely as Alice, was already gathering in her mind like an incoming storm. The Women in Clay would cloud around her with questions about What She Did Now and Where She'd Been, dampening the story she'd put together for herself.

'Were you at the women's shelter today?' Alice asked. It had already begun. 'What exactly are you doing there? I'm never sure.'

'Feminist Assembly,' Nicola corrected her. 'It's an *archive.*'

'Huh.'

Ben was right. To survive this she would need – as he had put it – an angle.

Her life, before the letters, had lacked one. There was the job she'd hated, replaced by the one she had fled. Orange linoleum, chloroform and glue; slowly eroding the slither of ambition stowed under her bed.

Now, it had a plot to follow. Each time she entered the archive, it moved forward. But how to explain this to Alice? Alice who knew where to go.

'We're here!' she said brightly, banging a heavy brass door knocker in the shape of a lion's head.

Women in Clay was not an official event but a dinner held roughly twice a year in the home of Honey Campbell, whose most recent solo show involved walking down a catwalk of unfired porcelain in stilettos. The catwalk had then been carved up to fit in the kiln, and the resulting perforated tiles sold off as wall hangings and ottoman drinks trays. Trays that *Vogue* had featured in a Christmas gift guide, For the Woman Who Has Everything.

At the door Nicola had to remind Honey of her name.

Before leading Alice and Nicola through a hallway of white floorboards, she gestured for the two women to take off their shoes. Nicola curled her feet in as she walked, trying to hide where the leather from her boots had made dark stains on her socks. Alice, in front, had been wearing sandals anyway and looked as though she had recently had a pedicure. Her pink toes smiled at the ceiling, happy to be free.

The pair were ushered into an open-plan kitchen where light poured through a glass roof extension held aloft by a steel cantilever. Around a heavy wooden table in its centre sat the Women in Clay, jangling together at an acute frequency. It was one of those unfairly warm March days where winter pretends to have left, and the large glass doors at the end of the room had been folded back on themselves. Tall wine glasses made rosy circles on the white linen tablecloth. After introducing the new arrivals, and placing them in the available space on the benches, one at each end, Honey gently touched Nicola's back.

'Are you *cold?*'

Nicola's arms were folded tightly against her chest. Made aware of her body language, Nicola tried to relax as a drink was poured for her and someone to her right asked her name, but the bench had no back and her shoulders could not un-hunch against the drop. Charred pieces of tender-stem broccoli with flaked almonds passed in front of her, then baba ganoush made from courgettes and chicken with crescents of blood orange, all on large, gold Astier de Villatte serving plates. Nicola took in the room she had admired from afar so many times before. She did this covertly, so as not to identify herself as a stranger. A Paula Rego hung firmly on the one brick wall.

'Arresting, isn't it?' said the girl sitting next to her, catching her looking. 'So empowering.' Nicola didn't think so. She thought the woman kneeling on the floor in pastels looked like her. She rubbed her dirty feet together underneath the table.

'Is it real?'

'Oh, everything is!'

The girl who'd found the Rego so empowering, Nicola soon found out, was called Eleanor, and had pronounced it with the stress on the 'or'. On the way there Alice had told Nicola about Eleanor's boyfriend, who owned a small gallery and liked to send other women photographs of his penis when he was high on cocaine. 'Basically, everyone there,' Alice had said.

'How was LA?' asked a girl in an oversized headband who, Nicola knew from her internet sleuthing, made 'confessional vessels', as *Artforum* called them. These 'confessional vessels' took the form of urns with phrases like 'destroy me' scrawled on them, and were badly glazed. Her question was directed at their host.

Honey said, 'Big changes, big changes. It's such a different place. You can't work in the same way there, you just can't. But you can *think*.'

'Isn't Johnny heaven? What he's done with that space. Are you doing Frieze with him?'

'Solo booth, Jem.'

'Fuck off!'

'Nic!' screamed Lily Topher. The Women in Clay were no longer bound to their seats. 'Benny says you're thinking of applying for the Ray Bower residency?'

Benny? Lily had long blonde hair and was swishing it, Nicola felt, directly in her face. Of course, she thought: chutzpah.

'Lily! I need a picture!' said another girl from across the table. Summoned, Lily left Nicola's side without waiting for an answer.

All around the room the women had grouped into twos and threes to do exactly this, pose for photos. The ones that had not were leaning over the dinner table to take pictures of the half-eaten plates of food and dangling flower arrangements. The next morning Nicola tapped through the guests' profiles to see if she showed up in any of them. She had not.

'I'm so into staging right now,' someone said over Nicola's shoulder. She turned and saw a girl in an organza dress, holding a vase of flowers up to her face. 'Take a picture of me in front of the Rego,' she commanded no one in particular, carrying the vase with her. Four women immediately crowded around to comply.

'Suck your cheeks in, Nisha, it looks better.'

'Put one of the peonies in your hair!'

Everyone was barefoot. Under the table Nicola wriggled off her socks. Holding them bunched in her fist she made her way to the bathroom, shoving them into her coat pocket as she passed it on a hook by the stairs. The bathroom door was closed but not locked.

'Come in,' said a tall girl who was staring at herself in the mirror, seemingly for the sake of it. 'Go, I don't mind,' she said to Nicola who was hovering in the doorway, gesturing to the toilet as she did. Nicola closed the door behind her, pulled up her skirt and sat. She did not know how to tell the tall girl to leave.

'You're Alice's friend?' the tall girl said. 'I'm Mila.' Now she was staring right at her. 'I liked your degree show.'

Nicola wished she wasn't looking at her so directly; she was blushing, stupidly.

'You remember those?'

'I liked them,' Mila repeated with a shrug.

'I like your earrings,' Nicola offered back.

'They're made of shit. Every time I wear them my ears bleed. Sorry, do you want some?'

She walked over to Nicola with her fist held out, a tiny bump of white powder on the flesh between thumb and forefinger. Nicola did. She sniffed it up steadily, urine still trickling out of her.

Tsssssssssssssssssssssssss.

'Thanks.'

Mila only shrugged again and said, 'I fucking hate these dinners. You know that Lily girl is my landlord?'

Nicola got up from the toilet to join her at the sink. 'I think Lily's sleeping with my boyfriend.'

'Who, Ben?'

The Women in Clay were still chattering at one octave below shrieking, shutting their mouths intermittently for a photo. Nicola cradled her wine glass under her chin as the woman sitting next to her explained how her engagement ring had been resized. 'They had to bash it down a pole to stretch it out, like it was being tortured!' Nicola's heart was pounding somewhere far away inside her. The drug had made her feel shivery and remote, like she was watching the scene from a distant vantage point on the wall. The woman in the Rego, still squatting among them all. It seemed that as time sped up she had grown; the purple of the fabric on her back getting pulled to threads with the movement.

'It's based on a fairy tale,' said Mila. 'A spinster lives alone with her cats, and in the evenings she starts to hear the wind speaking to her through the fireplace. It tells her to eat all her cats. That's why she's crawling like that, she's about to start.' She flicked the ash from her cigarette into a fruit bowl.

'No. That can't be true,' said Honey, indignant; this was, after all, hanging in her home.

'Why not?'

'Because she's young and there are no cats.'

17

A month passes without any correspondence, which is unusual. Susan, coming in from an afternoon at work to an empty doormat, doesn't worry, though; Donna always seemed to land on her feet. The boyfriend problem was just an unfortunate blip. But God, *Stone*? How pretentious.

She wipes her shoes on the mat and walks toward the kitchen at the far end of the hall, pulling off her gloves with her teeth as she goes. All with a baby balanced on her hip. She had just collected her daughter Jenna from the day nursery; the bank, currently understaffed, was keeping her later and later. She was the last mother to collect her child for the third week in a row. What she wouldn't give to be alone in a cottage, Stone or otherwise.

'Well, what can you do?' she says to Jenna, leaning in to make their noses touch.

After setting Jenna down in a seat that hangs from the doorframe on elastic straps, Susan lifts the stovetop kettle to gauge its weight. Full enough. She puts it back, lights the flame underneath with a match and falls sideways into a chair, waiting for it to boil. Jenna laughs and bounces and claps, now that they're a similar height, until the front door slams and she starts to cry.

'Paul?'

He walks through to meet her, shaking his long red hair from a helmet.

'There's something for you, I took the whole pile by mistake.'

He slides a fuschia envelope across the table, which Susan stops by putting her finger down on top.

'And how *is* Joni Mitchell? Still living on the farm with her Arab?'

She shoots Paul a sharp look of Don't, before catching herself and rolling her cheeks up to steer the exchange from a spat into a joke. Paul, Susan suspects, has never liked Donna, though he's never said so outright. They had all gone to school together, which can of course lead a person to certain prismatic resentments, and which Susan had happily settled on as an answer. The grudges people held onto never failed to amaze her by their triviality. If she'd interrogated the matter further, she might have said that perhaps this dislike came from how her friend now appeared: as letters, addressed to her, and therefore secret. Donna was not the kind of friend they had over for dinner on a regular basis. Even when she was with Dev and they could have done the whole couples thing, the idea had never occurred to her. It was not that she didn't *want* to share her friend, but that she didn't know how. Not without losing the sense of herself she had built without her; without tripping that self over and falling back into being sixteen, eleven, four.

Don't be a baby, Susan. DO IT. I promise you won't get in trouble, said a high voice inside her chest, giving the need to please a competitive edge for ever and ever until death do them part.

Her friend had lost a tooth first, bled first, grown breasts first, kissed a boy first, and in this way had always held the future slightly aloft. She had known, as if through divine intervention, how to tie ribbons into your hair to make it curl overnight, and how to roll a joint, and what a blow job was and the best way to give one and *God, Susan, just let me do it for you* as she'd wipe the eyeliner off Susan's face with spit and redo it in a perfect flick. Kneeling on the ground looking up at her careful hand: that I may catch thee up for I dwell in it! Even now, when Susan was certain it had, in fact, been she who had won the race to adulthood, married and with a nine-month-old while her friend flitted about a field on the edge of unemployment, she still couldn't shake the fear that this person would, at any moment, turn a corner she hadn't even seen coming and one-up her once more. The thought of this happening in her own home? No. This was a love that required distance.

And besides, Susan would argue to no one as she ran a razor up her legs in the bath, she was happy with what she had. She was. Yes, okay, she had done the done thing, but only barely: Paul was not a conventional husband. He rode a motorbike, he cleaned! Though who she was justifying all of this to she could not say, and perhaps Paul knew this.

'It's not a farm,' she said without looking up, 'and he's not an Arab. Also no, not anymore.'

~

It would seem my hand has been forced. Dev paid up a few months' rent on the cottage when he left (guilt is an excellent money wrangler it would seem) but I couldn't make the rest on my own, and honestly, I was going a bit mad out there in the middle of nowhere. So, I took one huge breath, packed my bags, and here I am! It was Rose's idea. Her friend Leonie squats an old hotel in Kings Cross and when she heard what happened she said I was welcome to slum it with her until I found my feet if I needed, and I do need. I am technically homeless, or 'in transit', as I told the dole.

Leonie is a potter too. She has a workshop under a railway arch nearby which she shares with a few friends who go to the Royal College, and is even applying herself next year. She says I can use the kiln and have a corner there to work, so it would seem everything has fallen into place. I have been invited into the fold with open arms so quickly and kindly I could cry. My life is already much more mixed and I am charging about day and night!

How to describe Leonie? She is very thin with huge eyes and cropped bleached hair. She smokes Sobranie cocktail cigarettes and listens to Edith Piaf and the overall effect is very cosmopolitan so of course I'm obsessed.

'Writing down secrets about me again?' Leonie interrupts as she sweeps plaster dust, dislodged from the ceiling, off a camping mattress. Sitting on a wicker chair with her knees to her chest and a biro pressed firmly to a page, her guest smiles and shakes her head.

'Nothing you wouldn't agree with.'

'Well, the heavens do!' Leonie points to the ceiling, which is leaking. Pushing her fringe off her forehead with the palm of her hand she gets to work on the downpour, a gold-tipped green cigarette hanging from the edge of her lips. A bouquet of artificial flowers sits in the open mouth of a disused dumb waiter behind her, framing her silhouette in curling cowlicks of washed-out violet as she stumbles about looking for something resembling a bucket.

She is like no one I have ever met! The hotel, however, is not wholly unfamiliar. Compared to the cottage it is the pits. Rotted wires, black mould, a broken boiler and – quelle surprise – windows that won't close. Remind you of anywhere? Yes, I know, back we go! The showers leak through the ceiling whenever they are used, constantly fusing the lights, and the wallpaper is peeling off in huge purple chunks. This morning – you'd never! – a gush of water fell from the ceiling right onto my sleeping face. The workshop is no better, it doesn't even have a working toilet. If you need the loo you have to go off and find a bit of waste ground in the square outside. Oh, but I love it! People are always coming and going and everything feels so fun and unreal, like a play.

'Some help, please!'

Donna puts down her pen and paper and squelches across the red carpet toward Leonie, who is struggling with a large silver serving platter. When they arrive at the source the ceiling seizes the dish in sharp consistent pings.

~

Down the corridor, in room 17, Donna's belongings sit crammed into a single sun-damaged hiking backpack. Unable to fit any furniture into Rose's hatchback on the drive down, the pair had ceremoniously handed everything built with Dev over to the flapping heights of a bonfire in the field, dancing round it, chanting about bicycles and fish. *A woman needs a man like . . .*

After Rose had fallen asleep Donna stayed up alone, watching it burn into the early hours of the morning. She watched until the wood had been reduced to white dust.

'Don't,' Rose said when she woke in the morning to find her still toeing the ash. 'You're breaking my heart.'

So, from one instability to another.

Well, no mind. It is a sunny afternoon and my bones are finally remembering what spring is. I've felt one hundred years old this winter, full of aches and pains and depressions, but! Things must surely be looking up. I was down for so long it really started to scare me, I suppose because of what happened, but also because I had set myself up to fail. So typical. Lusting over the conventional life; the garden, fish shops, chickens?! What could I have been thinking? In my heart I knew I never really belonged there, I belong here. I walked through the city last night, lost to the crowd, with everyone busy and bustling around me, their whole lives laid out in front of them and no thought whatsoever of mine. Squatting at twenty-seven. I suppose you think I should be ashamed, but I feel like your little baby, bouncing, ready to shoot up a whole extra foot into the world: totally untethered!

Everything is temporary and nothing matters and I am grinning from ear to ear because of it. What a relief!

'I could eat a horse.'

Susan stops reading and follows a rope through the dark towards the fridge.

'Shepherd's pie?' she asks the cold white light.

18

'No Ben today?'

'We're taking some time apart.'

'Heavens, well you could have *said* something. Dear me. I suppose I should make my peace with the fact that I won't be a grandmother anytime soon.'

'Jesus, mum!'

Nicola was standing in the belly of Big Topshop on Oxford Street. Her mother was visiting for the day, and shopping was the ritual they had formed for such occasions. Ben had usually joined them afterwards for lunch, to expound about his glittering career prospects and provide a welcome buffer. Loud music droned over the constant click of plastic hangers as they stood side by side flicking them quickly against each other on a rail.

Nicola saw her mother, Michelle, with a healthy regularity. Not too much, she thought, and not too little. When they spoke, they spoke about other people. Their communication relied on them. Specifically, their bad decisions, which were never in short supply. They would spend hours talking not about themselves but about why a person might have or have not done anything at all. As small as a look, or as big as a divorce. Nicola would say, 'How's Liz?' and her mother would reply, '*Well*, you know she's going to go through with it after all that?'

'Never!'

'I know, silly woman.'

Nicola didn't plan on going into any detail regarding her split from Ben Gibbs, just as she hadn't told her mother about moving from the nursery to Better Connections, and then onto Jobseeker's Allowance. As far as her mother was concerned her only daughter lived in London, 'Oh, you know, being a *creative* as they call it. God knows what that means!' Nicola certainly hadn't told her about the letters. She only listened to the judgements her mother passed and responded accordingly, satisfied that if Liz was an agreed-upon Silly Woman, she might not discover that her daughter was too. But perhaps she had. The grandmother comment was the first thing Michelle had said that day that wasn't about somebody else. It was as if she had sneezed suddenly, and now the glass between them was visible, smeared with disapproval. And yet it struck Nicola as cosmically true.

To turn her mother into a grandmother was to acknow-ledge the possibility of a future. Stepping out of a cold lake somewhere very far north, it was the one thing she couldn't do.

'What about this?' she asked, averting from the dark waters with a red silky top against her torso.

'Too young for you, Nic.'

19

Dear Susan,

You are now reading the words of a bonafide Covent Garden waitress!

Truth be told, the day before I started I could barely move. I was suddenly filled with all these horrible thoughts about going backwards. Always backwards, never forwards, back to the cafe in Hanley and rushing around with no time for pots and wearing my nerves to rags. The black cloud I managed to conjure that day was enormous, but I had no choice but to suck it up and get on with it because of course I'm broke . . . Honestly, work feels like a little rope tied around my ankle. I walk so far and feel free and like I might be getting somewhere and then the rope pulls taut and I have to retreat.

Anyway, my guilty secret is that I am enjoying it tremendously! When I am not at the restaurant I sit about the workshop picking my ears and chewing my nails . . . waiting to go!

J. Sheekey's is an oyster bar, no less, and it is always busy. Customers appear in a constant flow through the doors to eat fish pie, platters of shellfish and crab salad. The atmosphere is one of money, and therefore optimism, and the clink of glassware and heavy cutlery is infinitely comforting. Against all the clinking and chatting my mind becomes a buzz of table seven needs this and table twelve is late and table four are out of drinks, and I just whizz about like I'm on rails, completely forgetting that I have a name and needs myself, let alone fears. A tonic for someone as navel-gazing as moi!

Subservience really empties a person out. Glorious! I play a role for everyone I encounter and nothing about me need be articulated or fixed. In fact, the less so the better. I am adored and necessary to each new party that presents itself throughout the night, and never on terms more complicated than I am able to deliver. More béarnaise? Of course, madam, right away!

It is good for me. To be reminded I can play the part and be the easy girl. If anyone is ever looking for a confidence boost, waitressing is the place to get it.

'Chew properly,' says the man to his colleague. 'We can't all shit golden eggs.'

The woman who supposedly does shit golden eggs is sitting to his right.

'I do not,' she says.

Donna Dreeman is watching this happen from above the table. She is holding their meals aloft. As she delivers their dressed crab she looks carefully at the woman who is said to shit golden eggs: she is holding a bouquet of flowers.

'It makes people feel better if they believe you didn't try,' she whispers as Donna removes the breadbasket, 'otherwise fate is what you do.'

20

Jennifer Baines, of the third-floor bedsit at 23 Gough Street, is taking out the rubbish when she is accosted by Leonie, smoking a cigarette and looking like she hasn't slept. Leonie is wearing plastic hoop earrings and a floor-length silver trench with the collar turned up, so oversized that Jennifer worries she might disappear into it. Jennifer likes Leonie, and is always pleased to bump into her. She has what she privately calls Pizzaz. They exchange commiserations about the weather, then ask each other how their days were. Jennifer tells Leonie she has just got back from a CND meeting at another squat, on Gray's Inn Road. She hands her a Xeroxed photograph of a mushroom cloud bordered by photocopied cutouts of black and white skulls: WARNING – HM GOVERNMENT DEFENCE POLICY CAN SERIOUSLY DAMAGE YOUR HEALTH.

'I *am* desperately against missiles,' sighs Leonie, before being invited upstairs for a cup of tea to learn more. Namely this: the women at the peace camp are going to attempt to cut the fence, and, if she *is* desperately against missiles, she should go down and help. Jennifer is driving down there tomorrow, actually, if she'd like to come?

The next morning she wakes Donna by clacking open and shut a pair of secateurs. Donna twists her face into a sleepy frown of *really?* But Leonie keeps on clacking, saying,

'Quick, quick. Jennifer is downstairs and she wants to make good time!' She is wearing a CND badge as big as her fist on her right lapel.

'I don't know where it is, Oxford or somewhere, but did you know the camp is on a *military base*? To know that made it real. I thought OK! This is really happening. We have to *do* something. Don't wear that, it isn't practical.'

Donna, tying the laces on a pair of black plimsolls and being snapped at by secateurs, is supposed to be starting the lunch shift at the restaurant in a few hours. She hurries with the toggles on her appliqué cardigan as Jennifer, outside, beeps her horn.

When they hit the motorway Donna rolls down her window. She thinks of the dust balls that circle the heavy velvet curtain at the restaurant's entrance, how they catch the breeze and get to flee with every swing of the door. She imagines being vaporised. She'd heard that when the bomb dropped you wouldn't hear it, only see it. By the time the sound reached you, you'd be dust. It was the sound that swept you away. That seemed to her about right; that when the unthinkable happened, it would happen partly in secret. She had also heard that fired clay would survive it. Leonie, who'd just yesterday won a Robert and Lisa Sainsbury award to work on a new show, was talking animatedly in the passenger seat. As Leonie flicked her tongue in and out with excitement, Donna felt envy smack her so suddenly it was as if someone had hit her. It burnt with a ferocity so fierce she almost screamed for Jennifer Baines to stop the car, right there in the fast lane of the M4, and take her back to the workshop.

How could she have forgotten the pact she'd made with herself on those dark nights in Stone, to commit to the world of fire and force? How could she have been so easily delivered into indifference?

In her cigarette breaks at the restaurant, she had begun to play games with the businessmen who sloped out the back to join her. As they smoked they would assure her that she seemed so much smarter, so much more beautiful than your average waitress, and, given that were the case, she must surely do something else. Was she an actress? A dancer?

She would always tell them that this was, in fact, all she did. *Playing the part, being the easy girl.* The look of embarrassment mixed with pity on their faces never failed to fill her with a sense of one-upmanship. Now, it was flooding the car with gas.

Through the sulphur she hears Leonie describe the 'grave state of cultural health.'

'It's important, you know,' says Jennifer as she glides between lanes of traffic towards banning the bomb, 'what you girls are doing. Living outside the box.'

Donna knows she will be sacked for being there, sat silently in the back seat, and she is glad. She leans down and undoes the knot of rope still tethered to her ankle, kicking it under the seat out of view.

Needless to say I didn't go. I went to Greenham Common and got the sack. Money? Money doesn't really exist. The figures on my bank statements are best dealt with by ignoring their very existence. I will just concentrate on the fiver in my purse and leave the rest to chance, or failing that sign on again and stop fretting. And besides, Jennifer says that we should all treat our dole cheques and overdrafts as our rightful due. A citizen's wage, as it were, which is honestly how I viewed it anyway. If Maggie loves the banks so much, why not treat her like one?

So, it would seem I have principles after all! I am throwing caution to the wind and living on thin air, once again. Poor but happy.

Determined.

Don't make that face. They would have fired me soon enough anyway. A friend from the workshop, Joseph (Birk, son of the painter Henry Birk, no less) is taking us all to the house he inherited in Deià (which is a town in Majorca, dummy) and there's no way they'd have given me the time off to go. So there!

I am living outside of the box, and soon I will have a suntan. Women for Life on Earth!!!

21

It was a low, grey Tuesday, and Nicola Long was more asleep than it was. She knew full well that quitting was a bruise that sang and yet she stuck her fingers in and rubbed it to fruition over and over, against all the people in the world who woke up and made their lives bright; planted vegetables, hoovered, unpacked their things. In the attic of inaction, the monkeys stirred. Somebody had given them little cymbals, wound up: two feet, two three. Her head rolled into the pillow.

'Get up,' they said, 'get up.'

She turned their ringing over in her hand to read the number in bold across the blurred background of her phone. 0800 0640 4999, otherwise known as

Cymbals crashing.

How to explain to the Jobcentre, calling, that she had taken advice that wasn't meant for her? That she'd waved at someone she thought she recognised and become lost there, still standing with her hand in the air long after they had gone.

22

Two envelopes sit on the kitchen table, one for Leonie and one for Donna. Donna's has a note laid on top in Leonie's handwriting, saying Fingers Crossed! Donna walks straight past it and down the corridor of their newly rented flat in Islington (the squat having eventually been declared unfit, even for living outside of the box) towards the bathroom. With both hands gripped around the handle, she shoves a pair of scissors down the plughole. The sink had been draining slowly for days and only when it flowed with ease would she be in the right state of mind to address the contents of her letter. The scissors do not have the desired effect. She thought they would grab at the matter in the drain and drag it out in one long satisfying train, but they only slice it up and squash it further. Now she'll have to buy something to dissolve the mulch entirely.

In the shop the price of caustic soda strikes her as somewhat steep, but so be it, she thinks: it's what is required to make the rest of the day possible. If the letter contains good news, she will be glad not to have to unblock a sink in her newly unburdened state, spoiling the sense of relief.

If it is bad news, she will be able to get back into bed without the added spectre of a drain bubbling nearby. As she walks through the neat maze of alleys and steps that lead from the row of shops on the edge of the estate to her own home within it, she reads the instructions for use on the box.

It will endanger marine life and children if misused.

She misses her usual turning and walks instead, with the caustic soda stowed under one arm, towards the wealthy part of the neighbourhood. This was something she did often, as she felt sure – less a fantasy than a real concrete feeling – that one day, on one of these walks, she would see someone beckoning from one of the large bay windows. Beckoning her to come in and make it her rightful home. Looking pointedly in each she tries to decide which she'd be most pleased to discover was hers, assessing the choice of lighting and ornament. Her mother had called several days ago, asking her to pay them a visit. It had been a while, she'd said, and would she like to come home for a few days' rest? See the relatives, put her feet up. Donna had felt mildly offended by the offer and declined.

She thought about her mother's living room; the small marks where embers from the fire had fallen onto the cheap rug in front, melting the fibres into small compacted lumps, the trays they ate their dinner on. How far she had almost come.

Nicola sucked on a small square of chocolate, handing the bar back to her mother.

'How are you feeling now?' she asked her.

'Fine, thank you. Really it was nothing.'

Nicola thought she still looked a bit pale, impossibly small. Old, suddenly.

'I'm surprised they even let you give blood, surely there's an age limit?'

The corners of her mother's mouth moved down.

'I just mean – you're in your sixties. There must be some teenagers they can get it from, instead of letting retirees faint in the street. Obviously you don't *look* old or anything. They probably didn't even think to check!'

Michelle's colour started to come back with the compliment.

'It's these highlights. Oliver does ever such a good job,' breaking off another square.

Watching, Nicola was caught by an unexpected surge of affection for her mother, who was so small and so strange. So unable to admit defeat. She wanted to share something with her.

'Have I told you about the archive I've been working with, Mum? It's a collection of letters written by a potter, about thirty years ago. She was born not far from here actually.'

'Oh my. Here. Really? Where is she now?'

'She's dead now, she committed suicide.'

'Well why in heaven's name would she do *that*?'

Donna is sitting on her tall wooden stool, scratching the tallowy skin of her cuticles and waiting for someone to declare that the working day is done. When the working day is done it will be time to migrate to the smouldering cave of the King Charles, where she can order one lager and then another until the time speeds up into tomorrow. Today is a write-off.

But as sod's law would have it, it is always today.

As her teeth release the dead skin from around the edges of her fingers in clumped rewards, her pots, fresh from the kiln and the result of a recent excursion into slab building, crowd around her to watch. They have the twisted pale bodies of newly hatched chicks. Open-mouthed. Expectant. She already hates them. The impulse to smash them all one by one overwhelms her. The letter had not been good news.

From under her brow she glares at everyone else in the workshop, busy in their untroubled quiet. The radio plays faintly in the background. Deputy Inspector Ford has been called to investigate what seems like an ordinary robbery at Lord Cromble's mansion. It is three p.m., and no one is showing any sign of stopping. She pretends to be engrossed in picking dried-up bits of clay from a gouging tool, pushing the helix of metal under her nail where it fits perfectly, turning the plump end of her finger from pink to yellow.

I suppose I should put this away and go lamb to the slaughter to write this fellowship application, but if the Royal College doesn't want me I don't see why they would. Sometimes a body could be moved to think their work is a pile of shit!

Well, so what. Everyone else's work is a pile of shit in my opinion and they seem to get on just fine. Look at them all, tootling away. Miraculous!

Her head is heavy on her neck. She rolls it from side to side, listening to the bones that support it click gently in her ears. For a moment there is nothing. Only her body and the electric sounds of its small movements chiming manually inside her. Her blood, dutifully pumping. The dust carried through her nostrils on their bristly hairs. The cool, oppressive damp of the workshop and its rainy odour settling inside her. The boredom. The ordinary robbery. She breathes a silent groan, letting her chin fall under the anvil of her forehead. As if on command, from behind her comes the fracture. Its sound cuts the room, perfect and whole. A clean gag.

Crack.

'Cooled too quickly,' says Leonie, without looking up from her work.

She doesn't bother to turn around and find what she knows she will: her slab-built chick split spotlessly in two.

'It sounds like you're throwing yourself against the walls in here,' says Joseph Birk, emerging from the makeshift kitchen and wiping one hand on his jeans to dry it off. The other he runs through his receding hairline, which, annoyingly, she thinks, he pulls off very well. His leather jacket squeaks in quiet resistance as he lowers the fingers that have been in his hair and cracks his knuckles. He then walks the length of the workshop and places his hand against the grate that shields the railway arch from the open air, as if it were a horse he could calm.

'It's the storm,' says Donna, unnecessarily.

On their trip to his house in Deià Joseph Birk and Donna had slept together. Since then, she hasn't been sure where to place him. He had not been forthcoming after the fact, and she was not the type to chase, so the pair of them went about their business in the workshop they shared with relative aloofness until the number of pints consumed at the King Charles exceeded three. When the number of pints exceeded three, knees were grabbed under tables and the whole cycle started up again with an urgency she didn't yet have a name for. It was as though, in their daily dance around each other, their not-looking kept them afloat. Treading water, focused on the shore. When the alcohol came it worked like a riptide, dragging them down to where there wasn't any air. When she looked at him in the workshop, even out of the corner of her eye, she could feel herself missing a breath.

Joseph holds a packet of cigarettes up, to signal that he is going for one. Donna only shrugs in response. When he's left, dragging to the floor the grate he thought he could calm, she picks up a pen,

. . . resolved to ignore him and put in some effort. I am decidedly not at home feeling sorry for myself. At least when Leonie starts at the Royal College I can take her bench and spread out a bit.

It is unfair though. You know she's never even had a job? She has all the time in the world to work on being perfect so of course she is. I have half a mind to write an anonymous note to her parents telling them how much speed she sniffs

in our squalid little flat and have them come and cut her off, but alas, I am too good.

When she first told me about getting in I thought I would just die. Funny, it had never occurred to me before, but I could, I could just die. It felt very free, knowing that, you know? As if all along I'd been trudging up a sand dune with sand in my shoes, staring at the tall grass, and then someone comes along and lifts me up so I can see over the top and there it is: the sea: the sea and the waves crashing in. What a possibility! To just give up and join it. And in a way, to know that it was there as a possibility made it easier for me to accept my lot and carry on. How trivial, you must be thinking, to die of jealousy. I suppose a person can't help what defeats them but that, you'll be pleased to hear, will not be my particular undoing. Oh no. In my mind there are two ways to look at it: to think that she has an unfair advantage and always will, or to accept that my road to success will be a longer one and get on with it. I have chosen the latter. Grace period of moping not included.

In my moping I've been doing a lot of reading and have had a few realisations. William Carlos Williams says . . . Do you know him? Well, he says that there should be 'no ideas but in things', Susan. What I think he meant is that every idea should have the perfect image to communicate itself with, that ideas without things are empty, and he's right. I looked at my pots and thought to myself: they are the perfect object for my life. What with clay never being quite in your control and all but dependent on the kiln and its whims. One tiny oversight and that's it. Crack, bang – gone! To be a potter without believing that the future has a sense *of goodwill towards you would be impossible. Take the hope away and all you have is fire and dirt and a dead fox. So, it would seem I am an optimist after all!*

Anyway, sorry to hear about Paul. I'm sure he'll come around. I know you say you envy me all the time, but it really isn't the conveyor belt of men you think it is. And besides, nowadays everyone is trying so hard to be thought of as progressive and a women's libber that they forget how to actually pleasure a woman. A little bit of throw-down wouldn't go amiss! Which is all to say that you are not actually missing anything. And dry spells do seem to be an inevitable part of marriage . . . she says from her well of experience! All I'm getting at is that I'm sure this will rectify itself quite naturally, and fretting will only put him off and make it worse. It seems you could do with a dose of optimism yourself . . .

Why don't you come and join me on the other side, my flower? The sun is out over here!

Nicola pressed the page against her forehead. Grease from her skin made a small translucent stain on the paper. Her third eye, watering back at her.

When reading a book, if she ever came across a sentiment or phrasing that she liked, she'd fold down the corner of the page so she could return to it. If she remembered, she would then go back to the place she'd marked and copy the passage into the notebook she kept, filled with shopping lists and instructions to herself – things like Drink Less, Stop Lying, and Do One Hundred Squats. The passages she copied out from books swam amongst them as personal insights she might have had, had someone not gotten there first. Sometimes, if something struck her as especially profound, she would press her forehead against the page it was written on so as to absorb it completely.

Hello my shame!

She did this with the letters, too, when she thought Marcella wasn't looking. She had been doing it more and more. Now that she was, as her potter had put it, *sans man*, the differences she'd been forced to concede were shrinking. She had arrived in London. They were getting closer.

23

'I have tuberculosis! I'm finished! I'm sure of it! *Look!*'

Donna's face is stained with soot. It streams from her nose in two great fingers and her mouth is ringed in black. Leonie cannot hide her alarm. She drags her screeching friend to the bathroom by the armpits, like a body fished from the canal. There, the two women scrub and worry and wonder: what could have done this? Donna coughs and her phlegm is ink.

'A candle,' says Joseph when he comes over to fetch a book, 'you fell asleep with a candle lit. The windows are cracked, it's the draught that did it.'

He flicks his lighter and the flame waves compliantly.

'You really should get it sorted out,' he continues. 'The pair of you will freeze to death. The Royal has a fire going, let's get you there.'

As instructed, Donna dries her face and the three of them step out into the blizzard. The snow lands on her head like a cat's paw, padding her hair into a wet white ball and squeaking underfoot. As they walk she pulls her coat tight against the wind, in her pocket the worn down rectangle of her notepad presses into her side. When they enter the pub, the relief is palpable: it knocks them off the polar bear's back and sucks them into its innards, where the deep red Lincrusta ceiling looks ready to drip. Once they've settled in a row along the bar, huddled over fizzy brown liquids and dry roasted nuts, Donna takes the notepad from her pocket.

Where to begin? I suppose I should start with an apology. Sorry for the absence this year. I was so looking forward to our annual Christmas eve drink but at the last moment decided I just couldn't bear it. Not you, my flower, never you! But you know what my mum's like this time of year. Ugh, just the thought of clattering around that sad little house with them and their ways. And anyway, I'm far too busy. London living has thrown me into the path of all stripes of people. If you can believe it, I now count amongst my friends AN EARL. Harry. The Right Honourable Harry, no less. He came out to Deià with Joseph etc and is now a firm friend. I have been invited to spend the New Year at one of his houses.

I shall relish being out of the flat. Speaking of, you'll never guess what happened to me this morning!

Three days later Donna presses her temple against the glass as she watches the snow disperse. Now almost vanished from the pavements and rooftops of London, it flashes past in patches on the fields. On her lap is the most expensive bottle of sparkling wine she could afford, carefully cradled in a royal-blue vinyl bowling bag. She is sitting very still so as not to disturb the paper it has been so sophisticatedly wrapped in. Not that she need have bothered: when she arrives she'll be so uncertain as to whether or not it is the right kind of wine, and if it isn't what it will reveal about her, that she leaves it packed in with her pants. Throwing her arms up in a big display, saying,

'I left it on the train!'

But not yet. For the next few hours she is a duck, watching the sky shoot by in great panels of white and green.

When the train pulls in she is greeted by the cheery horn of Harry, handsome and waving, in a cherry coloured Saab. His hair, a bright mop of crisp birch shavings, blowing in the day. She hurries over and slides into the passenger seat where he smacks her cheek with country-red lips.

'Sooo glad for the change of scenery,' she tells him as she flips down the sun visor and lights a cigarette. 'Nice day, too. It's been *foul* in London.'

The weather, fresh and bracing, prompts her to launch into the tale of her brush with the candle, where the dark air had been the opposite of what surrounds her now.

'All around your mouth?'

'Yes, really! In a ring!'

'Good God,' says Harry. Then, 'This is us.' He flicks his head to either side, alerting her to the gates they are turning through.

A canary dies in the mine.

It is the grandest house she has ever seen. As it emerges from the trees she wipes her mouth reflexively, regretting the story of her soot-streaked face. Looking across at

Harry's lips she half expects them to be stained, too, from the kiss he gave her cheek. The house, standing in a clearing of dense forest, is dramatically stage-lit by the setting sun. Large rectangular windows look out from its enormous facade, catching the light in rippling flashes that force her to squint and look away. A person could be forgiven for thinking that inside it was on fire. As they creep closer the car wheels crunch across the gravel driveway with slow, almost solemn ceremony, as if Harry were driving Donna to her final judgement. I will not, she thinks, let the bottle in my bag sully me any further.

She is pulled out of the car by Harry's hand which then moves to her back, ushering her across that solemn gravel and through a heavy doorway. Together they enter a hallway as high as heaven and just as gently lit. Thick filigree and the ancient faces of great-aunts, naval officers and treasured dogs line a passageway that looks to her like a whale's back, arching above them in beaming bones. Joseph Birk is the first to emerge from the dimness.

'You made it!' he says, with uncharacteristic enthusiasm. In his calloused hand is an empty champagne flute, signalling he may have already broken the three-pint rule. The glass digs between Donna's shoulder blades as he welcomes her with a hug.

'Leonie couldn't. It appears that her grandfather, unpredictably at the age of ninety-seven, may decide to leave us at any moment. She fled for Dorset this morning.'

'How special, to be the only lady at the feast.'

'No Ruth?'

'Chicken pox!'

'Oh, well in that case.' She gives him a little curtsey on cue.

'Donna,' Harry interrupts, 'your room is first up the stairs on the right. You have the best view.' He winks and adds, 'Come down when you're ready.'

'Let me carry this up,' Joseph says, jumping to take her bag from Harry's hand. 'Do you have anything that needs to go in the fridge?'

'Bugger!' she shouts, 'The wine! You'll never guess . . .' Throwing her arms up.

'I disagree,' says Joseph Birk. 'What used to stand for the counterculture now counts as evidence of a corporate soul.'

He is talking to a man whose shirt, unlike his own which hangs lazily open, is buttoned all the way up to his swollen pink neck. Despite the discrepancy in their attire, Joseph is the one who appears to be sweating. Not squirming, exactly, but boiling over. Watching him, Donna thinks of how just an hour ago he was pushing her into the cold marble top of the dresser in her room, the one with the best view. Her stomach drops to the floor with the image. Joseph's opponent in the buttoned-up shirt chortles and jabs a derisive finger:

'You think a man makes a jug out of anything other than economic necessity?'

'A man makes a jug because he is a man! You are making objects that are so polished, so *pleasing*. I'd say there's such a thing as being too good. When the work shows no sign of struggle? Fine, you have a plate, a pot, but it's a dead one.' Joseph slams his fist on the table. 'Dead.'

'There are distinctions, distinctions. There is the bread and butter, and then—'

'Bread and butter? I'd say *you*, with your pig's trough interpretation of human motives – making pots is a life. You cannot make distinctions about life, you lose it! And you will, with your "vessels" and your "makers", it is gutless, utterly gutless!'

'You are walking dangerously close to a Little England Conservatism, Joseph.'

'Bullshit. You're deluded.'

'I only want artistic freedom.'

'You want your little teapot on Thatcher's desk.'

'And why not, why not if it pays the meter.'

'I cannot believe for a second! You will find yourself answering to nothing but modish tastes, economic weather and your own bloody promotional skills.'

'There is nothing else *to* answer to! You are describing the future, Joseph.'

Waiting for an entry point in the conversation, Donna watches them speak like a little girl stood silently in front of a revolving door, anxiously trying to time her step as its fast glass panels swing past. Her stomach, still on the floor, getting in the way. *Round and round.* She is afraid of being caught out in her stupidity, out of place amongst people she deems bred to belittle her with their Latin references and their projections from the diaphragm, *primus inter pares*, but

Lo and behold

She invites stupidity anyway, the afraid always do.

Under the table she cups a glass of wine in one hand and rubs the warm ear of a basset hound with the other.

She is glad to be near the dog whom she recognises as a fellow imposter in a room of wealth beyond her understanding. He half sits, half stands, ready to beg between her legs. The pair of them watch food go into, and opinions come out of, unembarrassed mouths with an equal fascination. Donna whispers what she has learnt about table manners to the fur in her palm, but no one is doing what she knows to be true. Everyone's elbows are in the drips of their drinks. The man in the shirt is picking from the chicken carcass, Harry is chewing with his mouth agape. Joseph just spat some skin from the back of his throat, a cigar jerking back and forth between his teeth. Napkins have been torn to shreds. Table manners are a distraction for the stilted who speak to dogs.

Suspended in a sea of smoke, the voices get louder and louder. Knives point at the word 'humble'. Harry brings the Soviet Union into play and the heavy bottom of the evening heats up. It strips off the liquid, leaving what one person might see as a good and rousing contest, another as a test of heart. She sits inside herself, listening, where the stakes of language are palpable. There is so much it can unwrap. Sign of struggle. Vessel. Pot.

All form and no philosophy, and I live in fear of being outed as a fraud!

'You've been awfully quiet all evening,' says the man in the shirt, turning to her after having shaken Joseph successfully down. He, at the other end of the table, is still rattling with the words Little England. Donna hovers her fork between her half-open mouth and her plate, looking around. Joseph stops rattling to watch. She sets the fork down purposefully.

'I think too much mysticism is placed on the wheel.' Her speech is slow and careful. 'I hand-build,' wedging the air as she says it, 'which I suppose puts me closer to a fine artist in some eyes. I think that's why my application—'

'Ah, splendid, an individualist!'

'I was trying to defend you. That there *is* such a thing as being crafted to death, that was what you were saying. I didn't mean to—'

'Of course not. Of course not. You were only making eyes at him to appease me. Only smiling, like you do. Fuck, Donna.'

Joseph is standing with his back to her and his hands on the kitchen worktop, having abruptly left the dinner table. His back that she thinks is so big and perfect, like a warm rock face, and that she wants to kiss, but is now knotted and tense and off limits. Off limits because she has failed.

'I'm sorry,' she says, reaching for him.

What he does not do is bring the saucers back in.

Her skin is tingling from alcohol and want, it is crawling through her *smaller, less significant.*

You know the script.

Joseph turns to face her. He says:

'It's humiliating, the way you behave. That dinner was humiliating.'

'I didn't mean to.'

'You never *mean* to do anything.'

'You won't even acknowledge that we're together.'

'I'm *private.*'

'It's killing me.'

121

'It's doing no such thing!' he shouts, striding past her towards an open cabinet. He fills a wine glass to the brim with red. She snatches the bottle from him and does the same. Her glass, overflowing slightly. She licks the purple streak from her wrist.

On and on, round and round, until they have drunk enough to fly off again.

Something like a rind peels off her with the minute hand. The neck of her blouse is gaping open. Her mascara is smudged and long tendrils of hair have fallen from the knot she'd twisted them into. It unwinds around her: letting the smell out, exposing the flesh.

As is the way.

If thou hast the weights.

She wishes she had Susan to show off to retroactively. AN EARL. A silent audience, an envelope, a time delay, a little bit of reverence.

Instead she can barely see. Beside a bonfire the man in the shirt sidles up to her again, dragging his chair across the grass.

'Shame about your application, I hope you don't mind my saying,' purring with the liberty of putting a hand on her knee. 'I saw your stuff at Waterloo Place. If you want my opinion,' chewed and swallowed, 'they look as though they were dug out of the ground. Very underdeveloped. The intellectual effort is slight when it should be asserted. *That* is their weakness,' turning the ice in his glass. He tops up hers as the bedrock cracks. 'Declan Fuller, by the way,' proffering a hand.

Soul ajar, she gets yanked open

– clap-bang,
The sediment loosens
and the soot comes back.

She awakes with a start at midday to ringing ears and the
nudge of a badly trained basset hound, who has pushed
through the door of her room-with-a-view and climbed up
onto her pillow. Someone, she thinks, must have put her to
bed. Her shoes are lined up neatly by the dresser.

The dog looks at her with his sorry pond eyes. Shit.
Hello my shame!

24

Shiny, unspoiled, tinkling in the draught, Nicola's day stretched out in front of her. No more grubby nursery children, their snot mashed up with bits of sausage roll, no more Francesca. Only the personal calm of her archive and the enclosed desk at which she sat. The almond musk of stacked paper, dust particles, lacquered cabinets and dry, rose light, where everything that could stain her was forcibly forbidden.

After showering at a still novel, unemployed-pace, turning in the steam and scratching the buildup of skin from behind her ears in soft, satisfying nailfuls, she picked an outfit. Without the sharpened eyes of a teenage girl scanning her sullenly, or the danger of pink poster paint swirled with glitter and tears hurtling towards her on two screaming hands, she could wear whatever she liked. She left the house looking a tad overdressed. The swell of cleanliness circling her in invisible puffs of fine powder, enough to make an onlooker sneeze.

~

'I just really understand her,' Nicola had repeated to Mila in a pub garden the previous evening over a bowl of chips and a bottle of wine. After meeting at the Women in Clay dinner, she'd endeavoured to get to know her better. Mila had, after all, liked her artwork. When she got home from that dinner Nicola pulled it out from under her bed and pried away the bubble wrap, gnawing her lip a little bit as she did so. It had made an impression on someone!

'You already said that. Here,' said Mila, filling both their glasses up.

Nicola continued to speak, inhaling as her pulse broke into a gallop. She liked telling people about the letters she'd found, she loved it. She loved watching them move their heads in disbelief at the litany of coincidences, too specific to be any longer regarded as such, that tied her to them. 'It *is* uncanny,' people often said after she'd hurriedly listed the similarities that were the proof.

'Basford,' she would say. 'Of all places. And clay!'

'Yes, it is strange.'

Their agreement filled her with pride. Evidence that something very rare was happening to her, as only happened to people in books or films. That the letters had been put there for her, and her alone, to find.

'Do you know how she did it?' Mila asked, taking a chip.

Nicola took a sip, no. She hadn't reached the end yet. She hadn't even been tempted to cheat, skipping ahead to the last few envelopes to find the inevitable played out. She didn't want to: too enamoured was she with her own reflection, of how good it felt to be seen. Under the concentrated space of a reading light, she watched with fascination as they squirmed into each other. The doubt and the dreariness, *something very close to dread.* She kept her reading slow and purposeful, compressing whole weeks into a single hour, connecting the dots in her head. She and her potter, holding hands on the edge of something, undead.

'I'd jump,' said Mila. 'Think about it. You can't have that feeling *without* dying. Falling, really falling. It would be your only chance.'

Nicola threw the potter down inside her as an experiment. Is that how she would have done it? She tried to visualise the particulars. Would she have gone to a car park, a bridge, or a tall building? At night, undisturbed, or on the brightly lit stage of day? Would she do her make-up beforehand? Pick an outfit to bludgeon? Would Nicola?

Nicola bought a coffee from a place on Lower Marsh. The street was just starting to wake up and the air felt fresh. She basked in her own perfume, mixing with the smell of her coffee and the morning light, as last night's conversation replayed in her head.

'And you say the woman she's writing to lived near your mum? Susan, is that her name?'

'Yes. Baddeley.'

'Have you tried to get in touch with her?'

'Not yet, I . . .' the Nicola of the morning flinched at her own hesitation. She must be quicker in future, she must think of something to say that will not equate lack of interest with lack of intellect.

'But aren't you curious? She's probably got her pots. If you found them you could exhibit them, alongside the text? The mind and its matter? Something like that, I can just see it. Lost vessels on plinths, open diaries in vitrines.'

'Letters.'

'Yes, of course. Letters. You really should do something with them. It would be a waste not to. Studio pottery *is* having a renaissance. I know you saw Tom's piece in Modus Journal. I'm sure Clem would love to help you.'

'Clem?'

'You know, Clementine Moreau. At Endo Works. She did that seventies mail art show. Oh, she'd be fascinated by this. I can't believe you haven't tried to track her down. Baddeley, was it? I wonder.'

Nicola had been curious, in the beginning. She had done some tentative googling, but failed to find any information on a potter whose details matched up with what she knew. Then she'd taken her quest to the Crafts Council on Pentonville Road, where she had been advised to speak to Agnes – a pointy young woman in snakeskin loafers whose professional enthusiasm had startled Nicola, used as she now was to the wrinkled, cryptic ways of Marcella. But without a name or even a potter's mark, it had been impossible for Agnes to get very far. Despite her well-intentioned emails filled with forwarded pdfs, scans of *Crafts Magazine* articles and leads to living women, they had drawn a blank.

'Try asking Catherine,' she would say. 'She was around at that time. Or Ruth? Or Tanya?'

But all of Nicola's interviews over tea and Duchy biscuits in North London townhouses had only brought her to the same scrunched-up brow, the same brief glance at the sky. Then:

'No, doesn't ring a bell. Sorry, sweetheart.'

The more she pushed, the less sense it made. Why, Nicola thought, would she have an archive, if nobody knew who she was? And what of her pots, the very part of her that would, by physical law, remain in the world after she had left it? There were mentions of them, of course, but nothing close to an image. No photographs or sketches or exhibition pamphlets.

'I mean, Christ. They find whole dinner services on the bed of the South China Sea.'

'Not here,' had been Marcella's reply. 'Only the letters. That's all I have.'

Only her days and nothing else with no reply.

'If you want more, you will have to talk to Susan.'

In the single-mindedness of Nicola's first search she had almost forgotten about Susan, the silent woman, whose details (name, address, even date of birth from the letters that arrived as cards) had been offered in simple abundance from the very start. In fact, she hadn't thought about Susan at all.

'Do you have her email address?'

'I don't, I'm afraid, but I have the telephone number she left with the box. Would you like it?'

Nicola had called the number and listened as the line went straight to a dialling tone, breaking the flow of her search with an abrupt and welcome dead end.

It was not that she didn't think she could find Susan by other means, but that she didn't want to. For there, in the echoing well of mystery, was where Nicola got to sit. Spinning in the darkness, singing to the wet walls. The lack of sense was the rope that held her, safe in the glistening black space. If the potter became a person, what would happen then? Nicola would be winched out and forced to work the fields of her own life, battered by harsh weather, and her well would be filled with the thick, completed concrete of someone else. But Mila's suggestion had framed the threat of expulsion differently. Now it had a name, and the name had a pleasing gilt. Renaissance. The word hovered above her head with viridescent promise as she glided along Lower Marsh toward Poseidon House and pushed its heavy swing doors, her coffee still preciously clutched in her hand.

She had been to Endo Works once. It sat like a spaceship on the bountiful, newly turfed mound of a demolished council estate. Inside, lacquered plastic wall texts carried words like Visible and Utopia into polished cubes of snow. At the time she had found it distasteful, but the cool disassociated halo of being in its rooms still scrubbed at something inside her, insisting on its own purified importance. She pictured herself returning, baptised in disinfectant and government grants. The image was not unpleasant. Still glowing above her as she entered the foyer, Renaissance morphed into Fate, their golden letters whorling as they followed her through the air. Mike Austindorf whispered from the other side of a symmetrical fold:

'Nothing is an accident.'

The green hills of Endo Works rolled out in front.

25

Shit, what a slog these past few months have been. Talking to animals like an unfortunate talks to God. You'll be pleased to hear, however, that my finances are improving. Alongside my dole cheques and the ever unpredictable pot sales, I have gotten myself some cleaning work. So, it would seem I have some use in the community after all! I am charging £3 an hour but that doesn't seem to put people off. And, for the most part, I enjoy it. You get to see all sorts. Best is a gay couple, mid-fifties, called Ian and Marcus who live in the West End. They are such characters I don't even know where to begin describing them but I will try. Ian is an actor. Marcus used to shift fur when he lived in Paris, darling, but gave it all up when he gained a conscience. Now he's a jewellery designer. He has so many tales, like how he used to make costumes for the girls at the Carnival Strip Tease club on Old Compton Street, and when he himself did disco stripping! They are very modern and cosmopolitan; they have a second house in France with a pool, no less, and João Perez painted their bedroom. Caring and generous too. Whenever I go over they seem more

*concerned with having a chat than anything else. I get
about a million tea and fag breaks even though I'm only
there for three hours, and all the while the cat sick just sits
about in piles! They're ever so fun, these chats. I like seeing
myself through their eyes, as a sort of free spirit young artist
type, and can make my career sound rather glowing if I
allow myself a few exaggerations every now and then . . . a
bit of vicarious living never hurt anyone.*

'Tea?' Marcus asks, poking his head around the living
room door.

Donna turns, a glass candlestick in one hand and a
yellow dust cloth in the other.

'Please. I'm gagging.'

'Two ticks.'

She puts the candlestick back on the mantelpiece,
which is mosaiced entirely in the shards of broken mirrors.
Above it hangs a gently rendered oil painting of the two
men whose house she has been hired to clean. Their
hands are intertwined and their eyes are cast down lovingly
to Erol, their black tomcat, who looks out from under the
arch of their touching knees with absolute un-cat-like trust.
To her left stands a lamp made from transparent plastic in
the shape of a woman's leg. It is the very epitome of glamour. Right down to the fridge, which holds only essentials
like hand cream and vermouth and never the dull suste-
nance (batch-cooked chickpeas, half-eaten tins of fruit)
that fills her own. The small roof garden, three storeys
above a Chinese restaurant, where they sit on white
wrought-iron chairs and gossip under a roaming jasmine

bush is, miraculously for London, always sunny. It is their love, however, that she is especially taken by: conspiratorial and alive with the sharp judgements of two minds formed in tandem, like magnets snapping together. She likes to feel it happening near her.

'We're waiting.'

She wipes her hands on the candy-striped apron she has taken to wearing there and goes up to join them on the roof, climbing out of a large sash window with a black painted frame. She blows her fringe from her face with the side of her mouth and, without asking, takes a cigarette from the packet of Gauloises on the table with the swiftness of habit.

'We sent Jan your *Crafts* write-up. She's very impressed,' says Marcus.

'Oh, but it's only a few sentences, and not even about me. I only get a tiny mention.' Donna brings her fingers and thumb together to show just how tiny, but her cheeks are flushed like an open hand.

'"The vessel's radical edge",' he recites, then repeats it. 'Radical.'

'Honestly, "vessel". How poetic. They're pots.'

'Well, we're very proud,' Ian puts in.

'Thank you.'

'I say we celebrate before you're gone for good.'

After my third glass it really started to settle in. I will be gone soon. Will you miss me? I'm afraid my last letter was a little over-excited and incomprehensible, so I will try to explain properly now. Remember ages ago I said they have that house in France? Well, it sits empty half the year they say because they're too lazy to do a holiday home type thing, so whenever they go in summer it's full of dust and leaks and by the time they have made it habitable they have to up and leave again. SO, they have suggested that I go out there as a sort of live-in lodger/handywoman/cleaner, mid August through till December then we'll see, maybe the whole year! I'll leave right after my birthday, which they're throwing at the French (I know, fitting!) and you're of course invited to. Joseph and I are back on (for the time being at least) and I would love for you to meet him. I think you'll agree, he cuts a very imposing figure!

The house is in a village called La Borne. Marcus says they originally bought it for the Picasso connection, but after a while they got into the pottery scene there. They have a friend, Jan (they privately call her the horny handed mother of toil!), who runs a small workshop out there. They said that rent would be free so they won't pay me or anything, but that Jan always needs a hand, remunerated of course, so I'll have some cash. And, if I get in well with her she's sure to let me use the workshop for my own stuff too. Apparently Jan says the French love the English (potters, not people). They're still a bit more structured in their ways out there, you see, so relish in the stereotypical British wackiness, which allegedly I have in droves!

In the narrow wooden crush of The French House, one week later, Donna is laughing so hard she thinks her cheeks will split. On her head sits a rangy mass of wire and plaster of Paris, encrusted with fragments of mirror and glass. The crown, courtesy of Marcus, manages to stay in place only because it is steadfastly tangled in her long crimped hair. Bodies surround her, squashed shoulder to breast, elbow to navel, ear to chin. Anyone who tries to move skids and slips, the contents of everyone's small wine glasses having sloshed onto the floor.

'More! More!' She claps and sways as she falls into Ian and he tops her up.

'Can you believe I'm *thirty*?' Her eyeballs are rolling.

'Try fifty-six.'

'Ugh!' She screws her face in pantomime disgust and he licks her nose.

'Cunt,' he says, then, 'Here come your admirers,' pointing his chin in the direction of the door, where Joseph and Harry are awkwardly pushing through into the crush of hair and glass and hands.

Her eyes jam back into place. She curls her lip to one side and adjusts her crown.

Susan, watching from the sidelines, taps her friend on the shoulder. Somebody to Susan's left steps on her toe, then eyes her incriminatingly from above a wobbling neck.

'Ella?'

'No.'

A cigarette tip burns her arm. She tries again to get Donna's attention, calling out excuses in her direction, but the noise coming from Susan's mouth drowns immediately in the air. Her tentative taps could be anyone's elbow, the underside of anyone's glass nudging past. The knot of bodies continues to tighten. Giving up, she makes a bid for the door. Mid-conversation, Donna catches Susan's black curls bobbing determinedly in the opposite direction. She puts her glass down on the bar, where it is promptly knocked off and smashed.

Outside, Susan is standing on the kerb cleaning her glasses. She takes in the air with a breath that moves her shoulders a little sadly. Donna offers her a cigarette which she refuses at first, then accepts. Together they stand in silence, inhaling slowly.

'Please stay a bit longer. I go to France in a week,' she says finally, moving closer to wipe ash from the cuff of Susan's camel coat. 'You can always sleep in my bed if you need to.'

'Paul will be at the hotel waiting, you know what he's like.'

Donna frowns; the silent inhaling resumes.

'Please don't go. I never get to see you, never ever ever. You've had so many *babies*.'

'One.'

'Please, pretty please.'

'You don't need *me* to have fun.'

'But you're my favourite person.'

She puts her forehead to Susan's chest and looks up.

Smiling now, from her affectionate height, Susan undoes the tangles of her friend's hair, working the strands around the tips of her fingers and out into the wind. She nuzzles her nose into the crimped blonde pile of it, taking care not to get poked in the eye with a jewel as she does so, and breathing in deeply: Donna Dreeman, soaked forever in patchouli, Marlboro Golds, floral letter sets and X, X, X, blotted in sticky blue biro. So much fine dust.

~

Well, what do you think? I feel strong and contained enough to do it, I really do. It would be an opportunity to work for myself and only myself, free from the pressures of recognition and the cliquey Royal College set. Just me, in my straw hat, a brick kiln and the blazing sun. I think the challenge will do me the world of good, and, more importantly, it will be good to have some time away from Leonie (who I resent and am jealous of more and more, with her stupid gold cigarettes and her trompe l'oeil). Once I'm settled we can work out a time for you and Jenna to come and stay, especially if Paul is still up to you know what. Oh, I really hope you agree that this is a good change and are on board. You know how much I need your approval petal, but I must say it feels different, what with being such an <u>independent</u> choice and not one, like living with Dev or Leonie, that requires someone else to prop me up. This will be where I strengthen my own back-bone! And it needs strengthening after all the upheaval of recent years. It's funny, I always seem to be on stepping stones, jumping from one thing to the other and always with the possibility that I might go down the river completely . . . well, once more then!

26

The 29th of April was the first day the sun had shone that year and the crowd descended, sweating, from every corner of the country, unequipped for the unseasonal heat and tugging at their collars. The small brick church expected to house them was equally ill-equipped. Its insect-ridden pews had been replaced with folding metal chairs, a supposedly temporary measure retained because it kept the building's insurance costs down; forty-two of them, it seemed, would not be enough. Additional seating was lifted off a stack placed against the wall, sending the sound of tight hinges screeching into the ceiling as they were opened. Over and over, until a man of the cloth cleared his throat and those without chairs made do. For those left outside, instructions were issued to prop the doors open; assembled on the concrete ramp they bowed their heads in quiet embarrassment as the sound of a radio belonging to the builders across the street found its way into the church. The vicar made his staid assurances of goodness and love to a room soundtracked by Jennifer Warnes, the audience before him, in strained concentration, trying to fend off the absurd.

'Leadeth me beside still waters,' he said.

'And I will dwell.'

Susan Baddeley said, 'Amen.'

When it was her turn to read, the radio seemed much louder than it had done in her seat, echoing off the vaulted ceiling. Why had no one taken it upon themselves to go over and ask them to turn it off? The small animal of her voice tried its best to clamber over it, stumbling at the addition of someone's barking dog, a distant car horn. A faintly gangrenous odour wafted in as the congregation fanned their armpits and the brownish water around the lilies started to thicken. Standing up there, she felt as she sometimes did when speaking to her daughter, attempting to answer a question Jenna had just that second been demanding an answer to, only now she was pulling up fist-fuls of grass and curling her tongue in two, making her eyes go crossed in the middle. One of these frightful strangers was wailing.

This was not how Susan had pictured the day at all. She'd had to organise everything, taking over from Alec and Rosemary Dreeman who'd moved about their small veneered kitchen like they were walking on water, forgetting to light the gas, pouring milk into the teapot, drifting towards a page in the diary they had all stained dark grey. Instead, it was an open door. An arch of white light through which the bright day was merrily intruding, carrying in pop music and the heady scent of trampled petals.

Leonie was the next to speak. As she passed Susan at the top of the aisle she reached out to gently cup her elbow with her hand. The briefest of gestures, meant as a Hello and a Thank you and, most hopelessly, a Why, all at once, but Susan did not look up. She was too busy fumbling with the pages she'd read from, trying to slide them back into her handbag without crumpling their edges. *Somebody*, her fussing said, had to maintain the sanctity.

The object of her slight had a different script. Speaking with a straight posture and an open chest, Leonie addressed the heat and the pop music, still lagging uninvited in the air, allowing for a little laughter and letting some levity back into the proceedings. Her eyes gleamed, large and affected, above the hazy beams of blue and red dancing at her sides from the stained-glass windows. When her heavy earrings caught the light she glistened. Somehow she was turning the sunshine into a blessing, the wireless into a sign of life. From her seat Susan watched Leonie's mouth move as if from somewhere very far away, staring at the eye make-up she thought too showy for the occasion and thinking of the words *who I resent and am jealous of more and more*, while a blackened knuckle tightened inside her. It had not been easy meeting Leonie – Leonie who had introduced herself, some thirty minutes prior, as The Best Friend. Susan wished she could fast forward to the day's end when, finally released from other people, she and Donna could reprise their roles. One doing, the other seeing. Cross-legged in their pyjamas, knees touching, she would explain it all back to her as she listened.

Was everyone very sad? She'd want to know.

Everything was slipping from Susan's grasp. Rosemary Dreeman's long bloodless fingers troubled the embroidered rose of a cotton handkerchief as she sat there, the heels of her brown leather court shoes hooked over the brace of her chair legs, like a little girl. It was dreadful, Susan thought, that she should be made to sit like that: on a folding metal chair. That she had not been granted the permanence of a pew. Alec Dreeman's knee was spasming over a trapped nerve. His old suit needed a lint roll. His low, bare head did, too. The pair of them, in fact. As if some terrible dust had descended upon them like a shroud, which of course it had. When his turn came, Alec read his clumsy acrostic poem:

Dreamer
Original
Notable
Now
[with a hint of bitterness]
Absent

At the mention of Doting, just before Radiant, Susan actually thought she heard someone snort. It might as well have been the sun in the sky. On the day they buried Donna, spring arrived, like a rupture in the firmament.

Donna's funeral was Susan's first. Her grandparents had already left before she came, and all other deaths seemed only to befall the very old. The amorphous facts of each, too predictable to count as anything other than the order of things: his second heart attack, her third stroke, the cancer that had dwelt above Aunt Doris like a cloud ever since Uncle Nigel died and she'd blinked her way from two packs a day to three. Susan was not oblivious to her luck, getting all the way to thirty-three without ever having been made to grieve. Especially after the birth of her daughter, when she'd felt her ignorance of the concept encroaching upon her like a threat. Those early years, when she would wake in the night with the sudden compulsion to check that Jenna was still breathing. Even when she could clearly see how soundly she was sleeping, against all sensible logic and her own desperate exhaustion she would reach in and lift her up, summoning the unsettled cries that served as definitive proof of life. And her parents, who in old age had seemed to only get hardier, setting off in their VW camper van for the South Downs with a tandem bike strapped to the roof. Something was amiss, for none but the accursed could sail through life this unscathed. Death was accruing somewhere, clandestinely, if only she'd known where to look.

When engaging in an especially fateful activity, like painting their planned-for baby's room blue, she'd indulge the notion. When she pictured her own funeral, it was as dark and grandiose as she'd thought Donna's should have been.

Well, she thought to herself, sitting on that awful foldable chair. Well. Here it is. My punishment.

The drag of metal against stone recommenced as people hurried to return the room to how it was, before being ejected onto the tarmac. In the layby outside the church, a logjam of cars was causing a small commotion. The formerly silent mass was now a gaggle; jangling car keys and agitatedly awaiting instruction. A hearse hovered impatiently in the layby, already edging its way forward to deliver someone else. Alec and Rosemary stood in its path, bemused amid the sea of faces that were slowly surrounding but not addressing them. From the top of the ramp at the church's entrance, Susan stood beside her own parents, watching the scene unfold and feeling the knuckle inside her tightening again, tense and protective. Prepared for war. She could feel, as sharply as if it were happening to her, the crowd of eyes boring into them, greedy for tales of cruelty and neglect, searching for some kind of mark. The telltale blot of a daughter who didn't want to live. Susan wanted to clap her hands and shoo the lot of them away: no scraps, not here.

There had been an attempt to obliterate *something*, she'd had to allow that much, because of what Donna had taken, and because of the quantity, but Susan knew her friend and knew that she'd probably banked on waking up, foolishly renewed. She had to have.

On the periphery of her sightline, Joseph Birk let himself out of the small iron gate that separated the church from the pavement and turned a corner, hands in pockets and a cigarette between his lips. Out of sight of the congregation, he kicked a dark green electrical box so hard that its door came free and clattered to the ground, exposing an incomprehensible tangle of wires to the street. Susan, briefly startled, turned in the direction of the noise before ascribing it to the building site responsible for the radio and returning to her rescue plan: she needed to get to the

Dreemans. She needed to apologise for the unwieldy horde of mourners and offer to drive them home. Sod the wake. When she approached, squeezing through the narrow gap between two bumpers, Alec's shoulders were held differently and Rosemary had her hand on the small of Leonie's back. She was staring into her eyes and smiling.

'I don't know about you,' Leonie turned to Susan to say, 'but *we* could all do with a drink.'

The wake was held in the function room of a pub with sticky floors and red paper tablecloths, where cumbersome coats were swiftly dumped in a corner atop another stack of chairs. Now with their hands free, Susan watched in disbelief as the guests circled the room, saying their own names and shaking hands to the steady soundtrack of screwcap wine bottles opening one after the other, and there, in the centre of it all, were Alec and Rosemary: joining in the rounds. Whiskies in hand! Drunk on grief and a strange kind of celebrity, they were feeding the crowd with baby photos, broken in the middle from being folded into a wallet, now smoothed out and held up to the light; the horror of their situation so readily displaced by that unflappably provincial need to please.

The knuckle in Susan flashed white. She pushed her way out of the red room and into the bin alley to breathe. There she found a tall man dressed in the appropriate mournful colours and whispering to a cigarette, with his back against the wall. When he explained who he was, the weight of his voice could have crushed her. Its gravity was underscored by the heavy black chambers under his green eyes. Not until Marcus had spoken in that deep dark voice of his had she known what it was she'd been craving all this time. For someone to do exactly that: crush her. Crush her with their sincerity.

Before she could express her desire to be smothered by a stranger, they were summoned back inside for what a woman with a child's voice had called out as *nibbles*. A distant cousin, hands fresh from the finger food Susan had chosen in her shock, smeared his crumbs on her shoulder and led her away from Marcus into a mire of small talk, damp with illusions to fragile minds. His self-satisfaction was enunciated in the words Health and Society. Susan could only listen, pulling a slow face and suppressing the urge to howl as another man, this one wearing a bright moth-eaten jumper and sandals, appeared to her left. The hair on his exposed toes fanned gently as he spooned runny coleslaw onto a paper plate. Life was serious. Why were none of these people taking it seriously? Why were they *eating*?

'AIDS,' said Leonie, catching Susan tugging at the tablecloth. 'We're all so *used* to funerals by now. No one can bear to be dour about it anymore.' As she spoke she waved her hands back and forth at the sad room. Burgundy curtains sagged above a stage where a hook had come loose in the middle. 'You have to celebrate a person's life, not *taint* it.'

Susan suspected other reasons. She believed what she could detect was not self-preservation but a kind of wild glee – one shared by people who had all committed similar blunders and had, miraculously, survived. When Leonie took her hand Susan wondered if she was on drugs.

'You know,' Leonie whispered, cupping Susan's elbow with the palm of her hand again, 'when Alec said Doting I thought I was going to *die*.' She jutted out her chin, then, a mannerism so suddenly like Donna that it made Susan start. 'Once, she put my goldfish bowl on the balcony because she thought they'd like some sun, then forgot all about them. They actually cooked. Their scales flaked off like pastry. Doting, my arse!'

Susan's whole body softened at the anecdote. Leonie was not a rival, she was a satellite of missing data. She had known Donna, and together, spinning back across the tide, they could piece together what they'd lost. All the tiny, inane details that render a person in full colour and hold them there. This time, Susan reached for her hand in return. Alec's acrostic poem had been appalling, the buffet was disgusting, and Donna had not been doting. What a relief to speak about the day as it was: insufficient in every possible way, but vital. Vital because now she was standing beside Leonie, and Leonie, smelling of cigarettes and patchouli, kept jutting out her chin. Susan apologised for not having spoken to her sooner.

It was then that Leonie told her about the letters. During the time they'd lived together she'd seen the careful way Donna had kept each one, and she knew how important they must have been. Speaking of which, she had them with her now. They were in the boot of her car.

'I just, I didn't know who would be coming to clear out her things and what they would take or throw away and I wanted them to be safe so I took them. Harry gave me the key. I didn't read them,' she added quickly.

Susan had cleared out Donna's things, as it happened. Just as she had spoken to the vicar and hired the function room and paid the caterer. She'd been sent on the instruction of Alec and Rosemary who, until their oddly giddy performance that afternoon, had seemed incapable of doing anything other than sit on their plastic-covered settee like two paper dolls. Susan hadn't known that Donna kept her letters in quite the way Leonie was describing, she'd never been so bold as to hope for *careful*, but even so, she'd been anticipating some trace of them amongst her belongings and had been hurt not to find it – sifting through the flat in a manner that bordered on derangement as the dead got deader with each empty drawer; the anchor loosening from the seabed as those on the quay are still running towards the ship, foghorns blaring, suitcases opening, hats flying off into the sea.

But there had been no need to panic. In the boot of Leonie's car sat nine shoe boxes, bursting with every one of Susan's letters, each as deliberately opened and undamaged as she had kept their replies. The knuckle inside Susan flooded with light. Maybe she was the best?

'I know', Leonie said then, 'that you probably want to keep these, but listen to what I have to say.'

With a hand on her shoulder she guided Susan down to the bumper of her car where they could sit and talk. She had a friend, she explained, called Marcella Goodwoman. Marcella had studied History of Art at the Courtauld, and was hoping to start a collection dedicated to the lives of women artists. As she said this Leonie nudged her elbow against Susan's, to bring her attention to their shared affliction.

'Now, it would be mainly ephemera, documentation, show posters, photographs, flyers. That kind of thing. Stuff that's easily stored. She doesn't have much space, as you can imagine, starting out, but, and this is where Donna comes in, the collection will also be for personal papers. Diaries, letters. Life. *Our* lives. So of course I just had to tell Marcella about the letters the two of you wrote. As it is, it's impressive. Who else could claim to have this?' She patted the nearest cardboard lid as if it were a dog. Obediently sitting on 'Sit': demonstrating her point. 'Obviously what Marcella's interested in are the ones Donna wrote to you, but I just thought, wouldn't it be great to have the full set? Both sides. You did keep hers, didn't you? Oh good. Then we have it all! The ins and outs of an artist's life, the minutia . . .'

Susan squirmed, then, to think what minutia that might be.

'What do you think? A de facto place in art history for Donna Dreeman. And it would be, I'm certain of it. Marcella knows all the right people, she's good like that. Think about it, will you? We can do this for her, together.'

Susan struggled to see what Leonie had to *do* with any of this, besides the fact the letters were currently in her car. She hadn't eaten all day, and the camaraderie she'd felt stirring moments ago was starting to turn into a headache. Now that what was hers had been returned to her, she wanted only to leave. From the other side of the gravel car park someone tapped a knife against their glass and she rallied herself for the long evening ahead. Before Leonie left she wrote a phone number for Marcella Goodwoman on a piece of paper and bundled it into Susan's palm, repeating: Think about it, will you?

She made it home around nine. Paul had stayed back with Jenna; his silhouette still where she'd left it, pottering silently behind the kitchen blinds. Before getting out of the car to re-enter her world of toothbrushes, tangled hair and bartering about bedtime, she sat in her driveway beside the letters Leonie had taken it upon herself to return. They were piled up on the passenger seat beside her. The reflection of the moon made a clinical circle on the car bonnet and the cuck-coo of an owl sounded somewhere in the near distance. The night, like her body, felt long and empty. So did Leonie's strange request. What *was* she going to do with all of this, now that she had it? Not read. The day had been too exhausting to finish with the sound of her own voice. She wanted only to sit. To be alone with the enormity of her friendship in its solid form. Proof that what had been thrown back to her week after week had a root:

Xxx,

Love.

She slid the lid off the nearest box. Each envelope had been sliced precisely along its top with a letter opener. She was surprised. Somehow, she thought they'd be torn. She ran her fingers across the neat open edges, fuzzy to the touch, as paper gets when it's been folded for years.

The button-down triangle of each manilla flap stuck dili-gently in place below: more uniform in colour and size than the replies she had in her attic. Brown, mostly, with the occasional stripe of blue and white. The stamps, which catalogued both the dependability of the seasons and the peculiarities of British honour (someone giving mouth-to-mouth to an Annie doll, a loaf of bread floating above the word INDUSTRY, Diana on her wedding day, smiling into an unknowable left corner), obscured by the inky wave of a postmark. What would it mean to give these all away into the care of a stranger?

For her eighteenth birthday Susan had been given two things: a silver charm bracelet with a clasp in the shape of a padlock from her mother and father, and a train ticket to London from Donna. The purpose of the ticket was for Susan to go and see the Thomas Hardy tree; bought with her earnings from working weekends at the greengrocers, Donna could only afford the one and so when Susan made the trip she made it alone. The famous ash tree, in the centre of St. Pancras Old Church's yard, was encircled by gravestones. They spiralled out around it, sticking up like strange pagan roots. The myth went that Hardy had arranged the pattern whilst working as a gravedigger, and Susan had made the pilgrimage to see it because he was her favourite writer. At eighteen she still harboured the hope that she, too, might one day become one, before her tidy drawer of chair backs and tea towels had silently grown into a home. That her quiet ambition never had amounted to anything did not strike her as sad. Susan was not a fantasist; she had known, even then, that the image was far-fetched and its loss was never really felt; she had found her outlet. It was sitting, like those overlapping gravestones, beside her now. How much she had enjoyed writing every one of these letters, detailing the ins and outs of her days, and sketching portraits of the people and problems that filled them. After seeing the ash tree she had walked down Gower Street and made her first and only visit to the British Museum Library's reading rooms. She'd thought them magnificent: all that domed golden air, blue teal, dark walnut, and walls, like royal barracks, of books. Marcella Goodwoman's collection must look just like that. Vanity allowed Susan to picture herself back there. She picked a letter at random from the box, edging it out from its soft casing, and read.

The knuckle in her breast twisted hard and tight, no longer light or satisfaction but white bubbling horror. There, in the middle of her sharp pointed script, the page had been ripped. The surface was scarred where the two edges hadn't quite matched up, grinning in the moonlight under an illuminating stripe of sellotape: this letter had been torn in half and taped back together. The ink was smudged all over from what could only have been large, burning tears. Susan read the page again.

I think of you often and I can't lie, sometimes I worry. Are you lonely? I ask only because it's a concept so far from my own experience, yet remains a constant longing: living in a foreign country without any real ties to anything. I wonder about the reality of it.

Rosemary is as demanding as ever. I go round twice a week now as her supposed immobility has prevented her from watering the garden and she complains of constant back ache, digestive problems, fatigue. You know more than I of her tendency to hypochondria, and of course there is always an article in the Reader's Digest conveniently to hand, expounding on her symptoms. That said, the sense of theatre and foreboding she manages to bring to such commonplace ailments never ceases to entertain. Of course she could always ask my mother to help, so I suspect these dramas are merely a ploy to get me over so I can tell her about you. I pass on only the good, but a word from the woman herself wouldn't hurt.

Jenna has gone entirely feral. Yesterday morning I was summoned to collect her from school for biting—

The rip remained. A keyhole to a vacuum for which no one had given Susan the key. Nothing hard to pick up and pry it open with, only pages and pages of her incessant rambling: paper, rot. *Are you lonely?* She crammed the page she was holding back into its envelope. She did not want to know what she'd said to the woman she'd loved who died. Died and left her with no one to answer to but herself.

It was happening again. The ship was weighing anchor without anyone aboard, foghorns were blaring, suitcases were opening, hats were flying off into the sea. Only this time Susan was not hurt. She was furious. With a fixed, almost trance-like purpose she turned the engine back on, clicked her seatbelt in, and reversed out of the driveway. How dare she?

When Susan arrived at the tip it was closed. Household waste was not a twenty-four hour service and it was now gone ten o'clock. Metal gates, strung up with chains and lit by the headlights of her car, made a barrier between herself and the line of yellow skips and tufts of chewed-up grass. 'Trespassers will be prosecuted,' she was told in block red on rust. But she had to get what she'd said away from her, had to make the bare knuckle inside her stop tightening.

She got back in the car and drove. Each box landed with a crumpled thud in the industrial bins of a single-storey Chinese restaurant on the side of a dual carriageway. Their contents spilling out onto the mulch of bird feet and bone beneath. A man in a blood-stained white apron shouted obscenities from the light of a fire door in her rear-view mirror, shaking his fist as she swung back out onto the empty road.

'She always spoke so highly of you,' Leonie had said. 'I think your letters were a great comfort to her.'

~

Standing in a doorway in the rain, eighteen years later, Susan flinched at the memory of 'comfort'. Beads of street-light bled under her collar, forming a pool against her neck. Intruding further down upon her supermarket pop socks, damp itched at the ridge where wet nylon met shiny black leather. A group of teenagers, absorbed in their own pursuits, shook the overgrown honeysuckle bush from the pavement as they passed, throwing a spray of orange drop-lets across her back. She tensed her shoulders in an attempt to make herself wider and shield the large plastic laundry bag between her legs from the attack, edging it forwards along the red and black diamond floor tiles with her toes, and pressing the doorbell again.

On the third ring, Marcella Goodwoman opened the door. One hand in her damp ivory hair, scrunching and unscrunching with searching eyes before the pieces fit.

'We spoke on the phone?'

'Yes, yes. Susan? You're early. I was just getting out of the shower. Come on, come in. No point standing in the rain. I must apologise.' Marcella swept her hand down to show that what she was sorry for was her attire; a thin, purple silk kimono with gaping Indian lilies printed on it and the outline of her breasts clearly defined beneath. Large brown nipples. The knuckle in Susan prickled. A bell stick of civet and cumin jangled in the air as Marcella gestured her to follow, with a wrist of a thousand silver bracelets. 'I'm going to run and get dressed and I'll bring back some coffee. The living room's this way, I'll set you there.'

Two cats with iridescent green stares emerged to make their accusations from the dark run of the banister as they passed. Susan followed down the hall, tugging the handle of the plaid laundry bag and waddling a little from the weight. In the aubergine light of Marcella's sitting room, she was glad to let it go. Rubbing her fingers from where the straps had dug into the flesh, she looked around the room. A mahogany grandfather clock loomed in a corner beside a pile of books, its hands frozen in place. On the windowsill a stick of incense burnt absentmindedly. The house was as bohemian as Susan had expected, but messier than she would have liked. Marcella returned wearing a similarly revealing white smock and carrying a tray with a cafetiere, sugar cubes and two handleless mugs. No milk,

Susan noticed. She watched as Marcella poured the coffee. Maybe ten years her senior, she thought, so early sixties? And so much hair!

Each took their mug and cradled it in both hands, waiting for the liquid to cool as an inflatable silence grew. Smiles back and forth.

Donna had died eighteen years ago. The number Susan had for Marcella was as many years old, and it too rang dead when she tried it. But they were blessed with the internet now, and Susan had dutifully searched. There she had not only found Marcella, but learnt that her original name was not Goodwoman but Goodman, and that she had changed it in the seventies. Sitting in her living room Susan found it hard not to revert to it, not from any kind of malice but only because she knew, and so it lurked like an earworm, threatening to pop out. She'd have liked to ask about it; she too had changed her name at the age of twenty-one, as every woman did after marriage, and no matter how many times she wrote or said it, it had never felt like hers. Now she was divorced, she was planning to go back to Bloom, and she felt this redefining of herself bonded them in some way, though she didn't dare bring it up. She found the heavy scent of frankincense hanging in the air and Marcella's braless-ness both intimidating and off-putting.

'So, it's twenty years you've been running the archive?' she offered instead.

'Almost, almost. I'm a curator, really. The F. A. is a bit of a side project. Doesn't get as much of my attention as I'd like. Mostly run by undergraduate students, but I'm cutting back on my freelance work, so hopefully that'll change. The travel, Susan, I can't do it anymore.'

Marcella rubbed her back on cue, and the quiet smiles resumed. The laundry bag lay on the floor between them.

After throwing her own side of the correspondence away, Susan hadn't given much thought to Leonie's request. It had boxed itself away with Donna's letters, untouched in a corner of her attic, as something to be dealt with another day. A day she imagined as having lungs full of sunlight, pushing open windows and dislodging sneezes with a birdsong of dust. That day had never quite presented itself, and, with the convenience of a thing not easily thought about, the idea was eventually buried under more pressing demands. Demands like, Why are there no more dinosaurs? and Why can't you make it like *Emma's* mum does? Until last week, almost two decades after the fact. Retired and with time on her hands, she'd been standing in her kitchen, baking bread and listening to Radio 4.

'Next, Janet Boyd uncovers the forgotten lives of four female jazz artists, and the tragic—'

Leonie's skinny blonde face, almost lost, reappeared with perfect shining clarity, bathed in the stained glass of April 1988:

'A de facto place in Art History for Donna Dreeman,' she said.

A sense of duty accosted Susan as the title music played, one that had been subtly working on her for some time. It troubled her nose hairs above the mixing bowl, itching as the flour sifted in.

'I'm not sure if you wanted her pots as well, but after Roger, I think his name was, died, of course a lot were left with Jan. It got hard to track it all down. I would like to keep what I have. But these, I'd be happy for you to take these. It would make me very happy to know they were of use to someone. I haven't been able to read them, I don't think – well, it's just hers. My life, I'm sure, would be of little interest. I've organised them by year, and tried my best with the order.'

'I'm so glad you think me worthy of their care, Susan. They're such a precious thing to have, we've nothing else like it. The quotidian gets so maligned these days, especially where women are concerned. It's a shame she never got the recognition she deserved, I hear she was very talented. She was close with Joseph, no? Birk?'

More air to the silence.

'As it happens,' Marcella went on to fill it, 'I've been helping put the collection together for the Catherine Koerner retrospective in St Ives.'

'Catherine Koerner?'

'His widow. He would have known your friend before they married, I assume, but it all builds a picture, doesn't it? She must have told you so much.'

She must have told you so much.

The statement spread through the air and onto Susan like a rash. Damp started to bloom on the walls of Marcella's sitting room, its squid-like movements unfurling with a rubbery urgency, dripping pools of ink. She felt the mug in her hand crack down the middle as ash from a bonfire began to circle around her. Two women in thread-bare knits with red knees and muddy boots threw tables and chairs into the flames. *Everything is temporary and nothing matters.* The light switch swung off the wall, dangling from rotted wires as the ceiling opened up. Bees swarmed in. Little saucers of sugar bent over a sink. Customers at white linen tables shouted orders over their fast hum as an oyster slid down her throat. One lager and then another, everyone so impossibly young. Church bells shook the branches. Locusts jumped. The extent of her and Donna's enclosed world was revealing itself in one great, indelible spill: *burnt to a crisp.* Two swordsmen leaned backwards, pulling on a bell rope while a girl in a lemon dress twirled, her skirt made a circle as she spun. A man, dripping in slip, stepped out from the body of the grandfather clock, a pleading body pawing at his feet before he caught alight and formed into a bovine head of clay. Hardened hands came to it from above, daffodils blooming in their callouses, the raspy pollen-voices sing-ing through the smoke, hissing their barefaced fact: that the production winding its tentacles around the stage set in front had been written for her, and her alone. The picture they had built together was not the one Marcella wanted. It was private. No one else would understand it. No one else could. It was hers, and now she was giving it away.

She tried to wade through the wet burning mass around her to remember what reasoning had brought her here.

What use she thought the letters could possibly have served when she was drawing up neat little cards for each year, marking each date with a stamp. A stamp she'd bought from WH Smith's specifically for the job and which she now felt a deep, protective embarrassment about. She wanted to tell Marcella she was very sorry, but she'd made a mistake. She should never have come. Too much time had passed. But behind the film of Susan's assault Marcella was already heaving with thanks, chattering cerebrally about the archive as a 'dynamic tool of production between the realms of the living and the dead—'

A cloud of dull, blinding dust with the word Dead. An ancient pile of papers dropped firmly down onto a desk.

'Common experience', Marcella was saying, 'can merge through the contamination of time and space.' Words like Repository and Haunt kept floating out of her mouth in clouds, to settle in her still dripping knotweed hair.

The knuckle inside Susan, swelling with what she had failed to understand, turned purple with pride in her throat. The colour grew elbows, firmly in place, unable to interrupt. She had driven for eighteen years in the rain and she'd be damned if she unravelled now. And besides, she thought, it would be beyond absurd to alert a stranger to the black pool of solvents, dyes and fatty acids still bleeding out from under her chair and onto her feet, especially one in the middle of a monologue. Especially one that had just said Haunt. She pulled a fitted sheet over her own stupidity and smoothed it out, waiting patiently for her accident to dry and for Marcella to finish.

'Thank you again, Susan,' as her heavy green door swung shut.

'The vice president of the United States, Dick Cheney, has shot Texas lawyer Harry Whittington in the face during a quail-hunting accident on Saturday.'

The sound of a television no longer being watched updated Susan on the details of its report through an open door.

'Cheney claims he didn't see his companion when he fired.'

She peeled off her still sodden shoes and laid them upside down on the radiator. The phrase 'peppered pretty well' from an American spokesperson found her in the hall. Curiosity tuned her hearing into the image. The sensation of chewing pheasant knocked against her teeth, those tiny silver balls of shot that stowed away in the flesh. She wondered what it would feel like to be peppered with them. Whether they would pierce the skin in neat, individual punctures like the even spray of a bloody shower head, or simply cave the skin's taut surface in one exploded hole. The idea of either drove a toy car up her back. Rolling her shoulders to rid herself of the gruesome rehearsal, she decided she would rather the hole. It had been a dull and lonely drive back from Holloway.

She rounded her head into the living room to find the sleeping body of Robin, warm with his own breath, comforting the sofa. The image dissolved her thoughts of chewed shrapnel and torn cheeks to soft mush. She was glad to be home. In the kitchen she poured herself a glass of wine, careful not to glug or clink any glass, then walked back to take her place beside the sleeping man. Pushing a bowl with the remains of whatever Robin had been eating, maybe yesterday's chilli, to the side of the coffee table, she filled the space it left with her feet. Another bowl, this one containing pinecones spray-painted silver for Christmas, glowed under the screen in front that was now turning its attention to the Winter Olympics. She jabbed the remote with her elbow to make the bundled-up athletes, red and blue against sign-posted snow, disappear. The quiet cleaned the room, breaking the only light from a streetlamp outside into orange points of shine and dust. A photograph of Jenna with her new younger brother became an opaque sheet of dark glass. Everything loosened in the dimness. With her head tipped upwards and her wine held aloft, she unfastened every button and zip she could find on her person with her free hand until she could finally settle, taking long sips of wine under her two-dimensional outfit. A clock ticked softly. The lids of her eyes bowed shut and she sank slowly down into the softness, before a squeal ripped into her back.

From the sofa her spine snapped straight.

A cry. Someone was crying.

Wriggling forward, half-clothed and urgent, she found a cat toy wedged between the cushion and her hip. Ragged, grinning and inanimate, it stared up at her. She tightened her hand to repeat its high-pitched squeak.

Hah.

What had she thought it was?

The sharp, cracked whine of a baby monitor, placed against the small of her back in case she drifted off, a hundred thousand years ago. She looked at Robin, but he remained in manly slumber, untouched by the toy's human noise. Its echo sent shivers of distrust through the room.

Teddy! Where's Teddy?

He told her he would be at Jake's (latest eleven, no excuses), but the shivers kept distorting the image of her son, shaking it up each time it formed. The DVD player read 23:05. Teddy was no longer in Jake's room, jabbing at the hammerhead of a PlayStation controller, he was bagged and sinking to the ocean floor. He was running through dingy alleyways from knife-wielding men, tripping on upturned bins and the legs of the sleeping homeless. He was alone and freezing, with a tag around his ankle. Lost forever in a dark wood. She stumbled through the thicket to the hallway, where her handbag swung from the branch of a coat stand. Taking out her phone she punched at the numbers, *HI. WORRIED.* She deleted worried. *HI. LET ME KNOW UR OK???MUM XX.* She stood, rigid, waiting for the answer that would calm the ground her heart was jumping on. The small square of greenish-yellow where it would appear glinted in the hallway mirror, illuminating her tired face. Her blouse was wide open, revealing two heavy half-moons of under-wired padding, and the top of her skirt had bent back on itself to show the swell of her stomach in shiny M&S pants. A small bow decorated their grip around her middle. The skin above, doughy and crinkled. Two large brown beauty spots and a dangling red cherry angioma. It was the pitiful bow that broke the spell.

I'm going mad, she whispered.

To revive the scene of Teddy at the PlayStation, absorbed in its safe, flat universe, she took herself up to his empty room. She found the nest unchanged, proof the madness raging in her head was exactly that, incapable of influencing the unruly expanse of night outside it: a stuffed monkey on a top shelf; a poster with the ballooning breasts of a Japanese cartoon, sheepishly signalling a desire for their fleshy alien counterparts; bobbly checkerboard sweatbands, a half-finished carton of juice. All surrounded by the thick, living smell of a teenage boy, firmly guarding them in his absence. Susan took the monkey down from its shelf and sat with it on her lap, rubbing the faded ears of its baby-bitten body whilst she waited for her phone to glow.

Seven hour-long minutes later, it glittered with unfazed reassurance.

Hey sorry getting a lift back now x.

All was well. Her mind sketched the angels of her childhood, reclining on fluffy thrones surrounded by pregnant grapes and golden instruments, and sent them a thank you. Small horses with sea-foam manes trotted around their floating feet. She felt like one of them herself, sitting on the cloud of her son's unmade bed with a satellite in her hand, tying her to him by an invisible thread of bouncing waves. This is how the angels must live their whole lives, she thought. Exactly like this: waiting for a signal whilst the life of the person they were sent to watch over beats in their palm. Listening to the tossing and turning, the changes in breath, until a cry calls out and they are needed. Needed because they have been chosen, and chosen because they would know. They alone would hear the cry and sail down on great, arching white wings, when the time for saving came. They alone would know that when a person said they wanted to start their life again they meant it. Bending its body in two she squeezed the monkey to her stomach. Its limp head hung dopily over her forearm as her own back curved forward, smothering it with a great incomprehensible heave. The silent rhythm of her weeping rocking back and forth against the small crushed mass of fur: a steady, stoic, private kind of weeping. From inside the throat. Then uncontrollable. She had missed her signal.

The knuckle inside her found its name and called out.

Come back.

To the empty night, Come back.

Her cry fought at the room, thrashing against the sides to find the chimney then floating up and out into the sky. Reaching huge and forever.

I'm sorry, I'm sorry.

Lurching like a ship.

I'm sorry, I love you.

Through the clouds.

Come back.

27

Bonjour mon chérie,

I am writing this to you from heaven! You currently find
me, pen in hand, sitting on the raised porch of Ian and
Marcus's château in the blazing sun. My ragged bones are
basically eating the sunlight. The air smells like pine sap
and there are grapes the colour of lime wine gums tangled
all around the stripey orange awning above my head. The
house is not so big, but it feels it, given that it's only me here.
Two bedrooms upstairs and a big open living and kitchen
situation downstairs. There's a courtyard that starts at the
gate and leads up to where I'm sitting, and a garden that
loops all the way around the back. They weren't lying when
they said it needed a bit of TLC, but nothing that a good
scrub and some beaten rugs didn't soon fix. The veg patch is
merrily sprouting back after a decent weed: tomatoes, some
kind of black cabbage thing, courgettes, and strawberries!

The village is ancient with romantic iron streetlamps and
houses with shutters that look like they're made of marzipan.
I can't say there's much of a scene here. Not like at home. It's
pretty middle of the road commercial stuff, pretty bowls to

put fruit in and the like. Tourist bits. Nothing challenging. But three workshops in total plus a little museum come gallery set-up, so plenty of life. Jan's great. Very much the tough, country craftswoman I'd imagined. Hands like an alligator! I can't say that what she does is really my thing but that doesn't matter. It's better than darkening the dole queues in foggy old Islington. I just help out in the mornings and then I'm left to my own devices for the rest of the day, which has been a balm. Honestly, I seem to have doubled in discipline and maturity without the ghouls of success and respect always knocking at my door, making me feel like a failure. Don't make that face! It's true. I am a failure, despite your encouragement (thank you, by the way). At least compared to Joe and all that lot. But that all seems so petty and far away now. I'm almost amazed at how much I managed to care. Needless to say, this is exactly what I needed. A bit of time on my own away from everyone to figure out who I am.

I keep thinking of my old college tutor (not Roger, bless him, the saint, but Graham – younger, cocky, maybe you remember?) Anyway, I keep thinking of Graham and what mean assessments he would make of me. He once said – and I will never forget this – that the shapes I make are more drainpipe than anything else. And that was when I was playing it safe! Well, here I am in the French countryside, tanned and lovely (kidding, I'm burnt to a crisp), utterly free of constraints, and I happen to think my drainpipes are rather good, actually. They are getting much taller and more experimental, some are even three foot! I've been using different combinations of clay and after the initial firing I smash

them up with a hammer and reassemble them using ceramic
mortar and wire, making them even more improbable and
twisted. You might be wondering how these twisted forms
stand up? The answer is simple. They often fall down. But, I
am getting closer to what I have in my head and I feel so
confident and full of it, I really do. They look very romantic,
I think, like something rising up after a storm.

Addressing each question one by one as she always does,
she lifts her page to check back on Susan's letter which sits
underneath.

You ask if I am lonely? Almost, and

A hot wind interrupts. Donna pauses, pulling the strap
of her sundress up from where it got tugged down. The
gust follows around to move the hair on her back and from
the bottom of the steps a wind chime joins the dance,
brewing a circle of leaves in time. To stop her and Susan's
voices from flying off together she places a nearby rock on
the pages and jams her pen into one of the pea-sized holes
that perforate the enamel table top. She assesses the sky. It
will rain, but not yet: the solid dark patches are still in the
distance. If she leaves now, she'll have time for her evening
walk, a routine developed to make sure she's tired enough
to sleep; the upstairs bedroom, fitted with an ill-advised
skylight, sucks up all the heat from the day to cook
whoever it finds at night. She checks that the rock she has
placed on her and Susan's words is stable, before getting up
and making her way out onto the path towards the village.
The path starts as dust before becoming a steadily paved
and plausible thing as it winds toward the centre, then
through and away in a fast stretch of tarmacked black. The

walk she takes every evening, however, forks in the opposite direction, staying on the burnt strand of single-track terracotta. She follows its illogical loops and breaks through farmyards and fields into a forest, and then up, out and around a small steep hill, to its top. Just enough to make her heart move and far enough to feel worthwhile. If she wanted to avoid the locusts she'd wait until the sun has set, but she doesn't dare to do it in the dark. Her short walk, therefore, is one beset by revulsion.

Grasshoppers don't usually swarm like this, being solitary creatures, but the summer's drought has scratched at the serotonin in their brains, forcing them to breed abundantly. The resulting horde of wingless nymphs are no longer grasshoppers but tiny hard-backed tigers, with the sloped faces of crabs. Baking on the dirt track in their thousands, they lunge at her shins when she tries to tiptoe through. She has not, in the two weeks that she has been there, grown used to walking amongst them. It is a sensation, she is certain, that would meet a person on their way to hell. Jan reassured her of their harmlessness, insisting the swarm would subside in, oh, about a month? But she finds that hard to imagine. They carpet the writhing path as if they were it. Only when she reaches the dull of the woodland does the death march subside. Rid of the bugs, her feet fall on the moss in soft, green silence. The bells of the church, marking the hour, sound alone in the air. She lumbers up to the top of her hill with wide, purposeful strides. She knows that the hill and the house at its foot are not hers, but she hopes the gift will last out the year. She hopes it will lead into the next. She doesn't want to go back to England. She thinks of the stepping stones. She thinks of the drain.

That swirling dung-green pool. She wasn't in it yet, but she had teetered towards it, almost losing her footing from time to time, and she knew how it smelt: it smelt young.

When they fired her from the oyster bar they had called her a child. You are a child, her manager had said, unfit to work here, or anywhere else for that matter.

You're acting like a child, said Dev when she grabbed at his leg crying Why are you with me, before he went.

Pobre niña, from a kind stranger at whom she had hissed, *Toma toma*.

Alone in the cottage at night.

Joseph Birk had called her a child, too, lying beside a basset hound. For God's sake, child, learn how to hold your drink. And later, after a worse display, simply: Get up, child.

It stank, then.

Could she? Donna wanted to claw the calcified infant inside of her out. She wanted to taunt it, kick it, make it answer for all its stilted ills. Drinking too much, signing on, falling down, 'underdeveloped', swirling up from the toilet bowl. Towering over her with four walls and a door, the alternate universe of Susan shook its head.

Is that what she wants? Stomping up the hill. Baby and husband and house?

No. She wants other things. She wants to make them. When she makes her pots she *is* a child. Brow furrowed, deep in concentration with her tongue between her teeth. And what was wrong with that?

High up, the hot wind whisks itself around her. Nothing! She shouts it from the summit. Nothing!

Below, napkins blow into the street. Diners at the village restaurant hold their wine glasses steady at the base as they talk. A tree bows. She grasps at her shoulders with her hands, cooing inwardly. Nothing, nothing, nothing. To the tree to herself and to everything. The wind.

She keeps on muttering, telling herself how to be and what to do, as she trudges back down the hill. Work hard, grow solid. Past the cows, the burnt-out blue tractor, the two dogs that guard the farmer's gate. The grey sky follows her. As she turns into the courtyard of her new home it opens with a God-centred crack and the rain starts to fall in huge, heavy droplets. Grabbing her and Susan's letters from the rock she'd left them under, she makes a run for it.

Inside the house she smooths them out. Susan's is torn clean down the middle. The rain has made the ink run, and the rip interrupts a sentence, but no real damage has been done. It can still be read well enough to reply to. She repairs it anyway, for posterity's sake, with a prehistoric roll of sellotape found at the back of a cutlery drawer. Satisfied with her handiwork, she wrestles her hair in a tea towel to dry it off and hunts about for a new pen, ready to take up where she left off, her previous one assumed lost to the downpour.

28

Sent on the advice of Agnes at the Crafts Council, Nicola Long was met at Catherine Koerner's residence on Pond Square by the solid stench of dog.

'Sit, sit!' Catherine scolded as a springer spaniel jumped up to make leafy-brown paw prints on her heavy black smock, bakelite beads clacking in command as she batted him away.

Nicola took a seat. The gingham tablecloth was strewn with hardened orange peel, spotted with purple wine stains and littered with old issues of the *London Review of Books*. Their faded covers, overshadowed by the scarecrow bodies of six large sunflowers in a tsubo vase. As Catherine boiled the kettle, Nicola surveyed the worktops surrounding her. Every inch was crammed with stuff: anagama fired bowls stacked with ripening plums, their sangria skin waxy with storm clouds, dusty Kilner jars full of muesli and dried flageolet beans, piles and piles of rhubarb, freshly pulled with dirt at the tip, scrunching bags of dried figs. Above, the reason for their overcrowding: the stacked shelving running the kitchen's length was filled crook to spout with pottery, all unquestionably by the hand of Catherine Koerner with her signature sandy brushstrokes.

'So, my love. How can I help you?' said Catherine, presenting Nicola with a plate of more biscuits than a person could eat in one sitting. A mug of over-brewed tea followed.

'I'm trying to find some information on a potter, Agnes thought you might have met her? The dates match up.'

Catherine creaked her matron's body into a seat to listen as Nicola began to explain, starting with the unbelievable fact that the woman she was searching for still didn't have a name.

'I may well have met her, yes. Do you know where she was shown?'

'Not really. She had some shows but, I, they're not really explained. I just know that she had them.'

'What about where she studied?'

'She did her degree at North Staffordshire.'

'It wouldn't have been a degree, not in those days.'

'Sure. Well, then she moved to London. She tried to get into the Royal College, in eighty-four I think, but wasn't accepted.'

'*Oops*. That would have been my fault. I was on the board of admissions then. We were a tough crowd,' Catherine chuckled, sinking her chin into its double and taking a biscuit. Her jugs and bowls hovering behind, as if balanced on her large, linen shoulders.

'And you don't have any of her work?'

'I'm trying to find it. She talks a lot about smashing things in her letters, so, but I'm sure there are—'

'Smashing? In all my career I never smashed a pot. Oh, no. No, the metamorphosis clay goes through when it's fired, that's permanent. You'd want to be sure of something before you fired it. It's serious stuff. You wouldn't *do* it otherwise! Smashing. Well. I'm sure she had a very nicely paved garden path. And she's dead now, you say?'

'She died in eighty-eight,' Nicola allowed, not wanting to add any detail that would subject her soul to further scorn.

'Hm. No. Doesn't ring a bell. Sorry, sweetheart.'

'But Joseph Birk is there, in the letters. I think they were linked, romantically, for a while.'

'We married in ninety-two, so what he did before that would be none of my business. Anyway, we shouldn't gossip about the dead, now, should we?'

'What about a Leonie?'

Nicola thought she saw Catherine flinch.

'Barber?'

'Could be. She doesn't—'

'California now, I think. Moved years ago.' Catherine then set her hands on her lap to indicate the end of their brief interview.

'You know,' she added, leaning forward to give the extra titbit she was about to deliver the required drama, '*I* never threw anything away and I've never stopped working. You can put that on my gravestone.' The scatological scrim of excess reinforcing her home held compliantly with the fact. 'I suppose that's us then. Would you like a tour before you go? I have some Hans Cooper upstairs in the study.'

~

When Catherine Koerner failed to deliver the potter all those weeks ago, Nicola was glad. The minute she walked in she'd known she hadn't wanted to find her there, buried in a woodpile of misunderstanding, where the embers would have smelt of boiled collard. Now she knew why. Fate, on Pond Square, was a word etched into sandstone and obscured by shade-fed moss, wet paws and wellies. As accepting of itself as the dead it grew over. For Nicola, it was golden and waltzing on polished floors, ready to bring them back. She thought of her conversation with Mila the previous evening. Mila had been right. She should do something with the letters. Something is exactly what she was meant to do.

Where before she'd had to press a knuckle to her forehead to find the light amidst the Honey Campbells and toilet floors of the world, now she could feel the hard compacted weight of her skull opening out of its own accord. Her dura mater tingling, receptive to the signs. All the drudgery and disappointment of living had only been a way of getting her here; finally clean, caffeinated, and part of a narrative. Prancing down Lower Marsh, pushing the heavy doors of Poseidon House, entering History. She was going to give the potter a renaissance. She was going to carry them both, she and her, out of the close red light that bound them together and into the realm of the living.

There was so much to set into motion. Finish the letters, find the pots, tell Clementine about them, Clementine who Mila had said last night would be Fascinated. Nicola imagined herself speaking at panel discussions and consulting on monographs. We must make a revisionist history of art, she would say from her podium. One that includes the Forgotten Women. One that includes me. The first thing she had to do to get there, the very first, was the simplest. Before ringing the bell to enter the archive, she sat down in the stairwell and riffled through her bag to find her phone. Her nail caught on the inside zip as she hurried aside used tissues, wrinkled receipts and floury food wrappers. Pressing her fingerprint into the black circular home button she unlocked her recent calls and moved, with a habitual twitch of the finger, down to find her. One ring. She bit at the torn down nail. Then at another. Spat it out. Mum?

'Hiiiiiiiiiii.'

Taking care to keep the tone light and gossipy – avoid the Why in Heaven's name would she's? – Nicola swallowed and began.

'Susan Baddeley. Well I *never*! Where on earth did you get that name from? Isn't it a small world. Yes, yes. Lived on Girton I think, or Valmont. One of those. Dewfield, that was it. Oh no, you won't remember her, moved when you were little. Lives in West Bridgford now, I hear. Alright for some. A potter? No, no, no she worked for some charity I think. Oh, sorry. *Friend*. OK. No, not that I met. We were never close like that. She's still knocking around though. Used to come to Rumba with me and Josephine. Keeps herself to herself. Oh, God, where in heaven did you get *that* name from? No, no. He went years ago. Strange man. Very strange. A *redhead*. Ran off with the neighbour. Left her with two small children, right after her mother died. Poor thing. She's got a new one now though, R something.

A phone number? Oh, I wouldn't have that. No. Oh, but I might have her email, from Rumba, there was a list. Now, let's see, where would I have put that . . . Robin, that's his name! What? Oh, no, no, it won't take a second Nic. Hold on . . .'

29

Donna sweeps her hair between her knees before she swoops it back up again and twists it into a knot. Gripped between her teeth is a glinting silver needle tool which she takes and skewers into the tangle to keep it in place. Now that her hair is out of the way, she is ready for work. She holds a tea towel over the worktop. Its belly sags with broken bits of pottery. She undoes the dusty parcel and lets the pieces fall onto the wooden surface, having broken them up from their solid form earlier that morning. She likes to use the hammer in the early hours. Crunching towards the misty workshop over diamond-encrusted grass and glistening cow pats to where, on the patio, she can heave and beat undisturbed in the frost. Her visible breath cheering her on.

Face taut, she begins to arrange the shards. Working urgently with chapped hands she slathers ceramic mortar onto their new joins, following the contours of their freshly broken edges with intuitive speed. This way, the fragments shape themselves. Up, up. She chews her lip in concentration. Spots of blood rise from under the skin to meet the air that flaked them.

She stands back to inspect her work. What does it want? Legs.

Filling her nails with dirt she quickly folds the form back in on itself, hollowing it out before it sets, and gives the next instruction.

Nerves.

She hurries through a box of discarded farming tools and bits of machinery, collected on her evening walks through the fields. Without gloves she grabs at a spoke to free it from its wheel, ripping one and then another like screeching hairs, her palms now streaked in scars of rust. Strange fronds. She works them into the form like whiskers. Weirdly delicate. *Freshly desperate. Not even pots anymore but innervated beings. Jan thinks I'm mad, of course, but I know their worth. It radiates off them. Without getting ahead of myself, I think this may be a watershed moment in my career.*

30

Nicola alighted from the Eurostar at ten to two in the afternoon. She was greeted by a light mist and a string of notifications on her phone: Welcome to France, and You have now entered your arranged overdraft. Transfer funds to avoid charges. Ignoring them both she opened a map. Clementine Moreau was not in London but in Paris, in residency at a women's archive there for the next three months. 'But if you happen to be passing through?' she had written.

The address she'd given was on a cobblestone street in Montparnasse filled with galleries and artists' studios in what appeared to be former shop fronts. Ivy tangled itself around the drainpipes and bird feeders hung prettily from the painted doorways. The sky above had turned to a gentle wash of purple. What was the word for it, that disappointment people felt upon visiting Paris and finding it wanting. Nicola couldn't recall, but whatever it was, as she rang the buzzer and a cat curled itself around her shin, was gladly not happening to her. Arranged on Clementine's table especially for her visit was a platter, a sort of picnic: olives sitting in their brine in a retro-looking tin can, tiny cubes of Comté with the rind sliced off, marble ribbons of thinly sliced cured ham. Smiling hello, a glass of wine was poured for her, fizzy and red, in an elegant thimble of a glass.

'Please, help yourself. I don't have long I'm afraid, but when you said you were passing through, I just thought *oh!* Oh, why *not?* I have to leave for an opening in an hour, I hope that's alright?'

Nicola nodded her head.

'It's Honey Campbell's exposition, you're welcome to join. Do you know her work?'

Swallowing a cube of cheese, 'I was at her last dinner, for Women in Clay.'

'Oh! Oh, then it all makes sense now. Oh, well in *that* case,' topping up Nicola's glass, 'So you say you've been working with some letters?'

Nicola arrived back at the Airbnb just after midnight. She arranged her little wares, collected from the day, neatly upon a side table; a folded poster from Honey's show, Clementine's book, her used metro tickets. A bird watched her from the windowsill, bluish, with a long, light copper tail. Its song was a quiet crackling sound, like cellophane being scrunched.

31

The ends snap easily, just as Jan has taught her. Far easier than lining them up one by one before a knife as her mother had done. She drops each bean confidently into the bowl beneath her wrist, feeling their short hairs flick against the hard skin of her fingertips as she goes. Their sweet, broken smell opening with each crack. *I am so much braver now*, she thinks as the pile grows. Crunching one in her mouth, she pictures the work she collected from the kiln that morning. It had been her favourite yet.

'Two out of four,' Jan shouted from inside the workshop as Donna flung open the top half of the stable door, sending bits of wood, brick and frost flickering into the air. She leant her forearms on the splintered lower half in a bunched-up sulk.

'You can't be surprised. It's difficult, what you're trying to do. Two out of four is *good*,' pushed Jan, 'better than last time.' Her voice squinted uncharacteristically in the attempt at an encouraging note. Jan didn't quite understand the shapes the young woman in front of her managed to wrestle into the universe, but she liked them, would even go so far as to say she found their unweaned elegance, occasionally, quite moving. 'This one came out very well,' she said as Donna circled the spoils of her hands. 'Like a fawn.'

'A fawn? Do you think, Jan? Ooh, I like that.'

Donna leant against the table and took her pot in both hands, bending her knees slightly to bring her to its level. She surveyed it closely, like a person inspecting the eyes of a child to check if they are telling the truth.

'Yes,' she confirmed finally, pleased. 'Like a fawn.'

'I know what I'm doing now, don't I?' She says this out loud to Marmalade, the cat, who is lying between her feet. His ears twitch from the depths of his dozing, before the kitchen door pushes open and he scrambles off with clicking paws. The fog it had been holding off tumbles in after him. In the icy bright slit of the open door, rigid as the frame itself, stands Jan. Her face is contorted in a way Donna hasn't seen before; like someone had covered her features in candle wax, then scratched all the wrinkles in afresh.

'I've just spoken to Marcus,' she says, pulling out a chair to sit in the dim stone alcove by the door; her calloused hands too strong and gruff for her, as they jerk it with a screech across the tiles. Donna stands by the sink, staring, the body of a French bean in one hand and its broken tip in the other. Jan, with her strange new eyes fixed on the floor, recounts what Marcus told her on the phone. In slow and certain terms, she explains what happened to the best of her knowledge, the order of events, when and how: yesterday evening, Ian, turning out of Savoy Street and crossing the Strand, had been hit by a taxi. There was swelling on the brain. He'd had emergency surgery but did not survive the night.

In the days following, it feels to Donna as though the very air has lost its character. Where before the cold had seemed fresh and new, making the grass sparkle and her days unfold with a kind of metallic purpose, now it seems miserable and heavy. It squats somewhere sodden in her knees, and she no longer knows how to move unthinkingly through it. She has no idea how to comfort Jan; she hasn't known her very long, she reasons, not really, not in the grand scheme of things, so how can she know what she needs? Instead she avoids her, retreating further and further into the house and its hard walls. She paces it, running her hands along the iron bed frames and the stone bricks which turn her fingertips to bone, sleeping fitfully in the barren doily of a bedroom at the top. Waiting, one, two, three days to call Marcus, as Jan had told her to. Because of the shock. Her wait is spent scrubbing the floors and the sinks with wire wool, her hands thrusting furiously, as if crawling away from herself in a desperate attempt at both visible gratitude and outright apology. She knows her days there are numbered. When Jan had broken the news her first thought had not been for Marcus, left suddenly loveless at the door to old age, but for herself: he would make her leave, she knew it. She didn't want to. The scrubbing set the guilt into a seesaw.

Not fair, not fair, no, no, *no. I am sorry and selfish for saying it but it's true. Everything feels suddenly very unreal, like I have been spinning around very quickly and someone has just let go. I really felt things were starting to open up for me here. I mean, not that I would want to stay here in any permanent sense, but that what I was doing here was getting me ready to return. And I'm not ready. It's like someone had turned the volume down on London and I had some quiet to get all my wants and needs in order, but now someone has just barged in and turned it back up and everything is unravelling all over. I felt so grubby and grey and trapped at home, and I can't bear the thought of going back before I'm ready. I nearly am, but not yet.*

On the phone Marcus said he's selling the Soho flat. It was Ian's and it's not certain who will get it, because I suppose in the eyes of the law there isn't anything to tie Marcus to it, even though he lived there and made it so perfect and it's his home. This house is in his name, and his alone, so he will need it back. He said I could stay out the month if I wanted, but the funeral will be on the 22nd so if I want to go I should leave with Jan on Friday, which I will, of course, I wouldn't dream of doing otherwise. Then I guess I'll just stay in London. I'm going to leave everything I've made here, and then figure out a way to get it to England later – it would be too expensive to go back and forth collecting it myself, and anyway I don't dare do the drive alone.

It is crushing, though. I've been so calm and happy here. Truth be told, I have never felt more like myself. Clear-headed. And I'm so proud of the work I've made. It feels so inevitable that when I leave everything will just go back to

184

how it was, cleaning houses and chasing after Joe and never getting anything, never ever, always just getting passed over and ignored. I wish this wasn't happening. I don't even have anywhere to live when I get back. And of course all this is my own fault for existing on the handouts of other people always and not trying to build anything of my own. The way that London had got for me – working endless silly jobs, then spending all my free time tearing my hair out in the fucking pub. I know I will have to bring some of the resolve I have learnt here back with me, structure, routine, being good about drinking, just the one glass of wine an evening etc, but it's so hard isn't it? When the city is set on eating you.

God, I do mourn Ian I do. I think I am just in shock.

Want to hear something that'll make your hair curl and me look less bad? I called Helen today, remember her? From Bambury Ave.? Anyway I called her up because she owes me some money (which I need) and you know what she said? She said: And to think you cleaned his house. *Really. Can you believe it? He was hit by a bloody car! It just goes to show you how thick and prejudiced everyone is. The world's going to dogshit, I'm sure of it.*

32

If Susan leant her body to the left she could rest her forehead on the wall. She pressed into it, letting the plaster
cool her skin. In the decade that passed no one had asked
her to account for where she had left Donna and why, at
sixty-three, she thought she might have avoided the task
entirely. She'd kept an eye on Marcella's archive over the
years, and she knew, from a brief check of its website every
so often, that it was in trouble. She'd read the pleas to save
it and seen the petitions. The list of signatures was always
pitiful. There, at least, Donna could rest in peace. No one,
she assured herself, was ever going to read her letters. Her
chair rotated forty-five degrees as she rolled her body back
across the wall with the top of her head to face the screen.
She'd also seen, in her tentative snooping on the archive's
website, that the letters had been catalogued not under
Donna's name but hers, and who would ever ask to read
that? But there it was, on the screen, in her inbox.

Subject: The Susan Baddeley Papers.

She rapped her knuckles on the plastic back of the
computer mouse which hovered over the line. Two flat

cloven buttons stuck out from its tapered head. More like a pig's foot than a rodent's body, she thought, now that the wire of its tail had been made obsolete. If she tapped the left toe, the email would open. She dragged it to the opposite corner instead, clicking the small apple icon that sent the whole contraption to sleep, and got up. The garden needed doing.

She unwound the hose from the hook where it lived, beside what used to be an outhouse and now contained a washing machine, a floral bag of clothes pegs and an old fridge, filled with bottles of slimline Schweppes for her and beers for the boys. Its rubber green body fell against the decking in a loose coil, bouncing like a live thing and dribbling lewdly from its tip. She kicked it onto the lawn and turned the tap, watching it uncurl into a long and writhing line. Its spurting head, flicking from left to right. A hunter in pink Havaianas flip-flops, she crept across the grass to steady it by the neck, catching it with her left hand. The creature calmed and the water curved, adopting its familiar suburban silhouette. A neat arch from hand to plant.

She would never, she thought, as she sprayed the honeysuckle, have shown Donna's letters to anyone had Leonie not suggested it. They would have stayed in her attic, undisturbed, probably, until she died. But Donna so desperately wanted to be known, and the bargain was that if Marcella had a say in it she might be. She looked down. Tiny droplets of water ran around her foot before jumping off with a shake of the ankle. Letting the water droop from its crescent momentarily, Susan caught her stomach intruding on her field of vision. She sucked it in on instinct, then breathed out to let it bob freely again. She used to hate the so-called spare tyre that had become of her waist but now she almost didn't care. She'd even, in her more private moments, come to love it. She felt it gave her sex life more colour. When she fucked Robin her whole body *moved*. It was incredible. She'd always been so rakish before, so sharp. But, her thoughts pushed in to finish what they'd started, she had gone to Marcella too late. By the time she arrived, Donna's contemporaries had long overtaken her to become big names in glass cases, leaving her friend as little but a footnote. If she'd been quicker, Donna might have been able to cling onto their coat tails and join them, pulled out of the grave by association. But she had not. And so Donna remained as she was: reckoning quietly underneath them, with the daffodil bulbs and the dirt. She pictured Marcella all those years ago, sitting in her house in Holloway, asking not about the quality of the ground but about *Catherine Koerner.* Some Feminist Assembly, Susan thought. She let the hose drop down into the grass where it continued its struggle of jerks and twists until she turned it off at the wall.

But what do I know? she asked herself, as the body behind her relented.

She took a small can of tonic water from the old fridge in the outhouse and carried it through open French doors into the kitchen, where its gleaming silver replacement stood six feet high. Ice fell into her glass from the frosted tray. As she squeezed a lime over the ice the wick of her nail winced from where it had torn the day before, then a double measure of gin went in. She sucked her stinging finger and carried the drink back out onto the decking to sit herself down on a garden chair.

Not much, was the answer she gave herself, taking a sip.

She looked out across the freshly watered garden and lit a cigarette from the packet she kept hidden in the bag of clothes pegs.

Not much at all.

But perhaps this email had a different agenda. Perhaps this person *would* like to know about the daffodils and the dirt. If they did, what would she tell them? Taking a drag she watched the smoke billow out in front, stretching out through the air in a long rope. She'd have to tell them about herself. She'd have to tell them about how unhappy a person can be without even knowing it. So unhappy that she'd read the words of her dying friend only in opposition to herself. They'd spoken to her in a voice she invented, one that was excitable and upbeat, *no less*, jumping from one stone to the next with blonde cheeks chiming about parties and plonk. Worry scattered only lightly, like dust or bees. When she'd cleared out Donna's belongings from the flat she had died in and seen it: the uneaten meals creeping with mould, their plates dashed with cigarette butts and strewn across the bed, a bed which anyone who was sleeping regularly if at all would not have been able to use, she'd seen how crooked that thing was. Friendship. How hard you had to listen through the static of your own feedback for the truth of it. How if you weren't careful the distortion could shift dimensions ever so slightly, make a death look like a life. How easy it was to read something wrong.

For years after she would wake in a cold sweat, heart thumping. It was especially bad on holiday, sleeping in foreign rooms, already disorientated. The fear that woke her was that Donna was still alive somewhere.

Who, then, did we bury? Twice it made her physically sick.

Write it down, she'd been told by a therapist, to get your dreams in order. And so that is what she'd had to do – of all things – write 'Donna died' on a scrap of paper, on a Greek island, in the middle of the night.

If she'd been happy then, as she was now, would she have understood it all better? The rope frayed in the air and broke. She suspected not. The thought saddened her. Taking another sip of her drink she felt the sugar and acid prickle on her tongue as it passed over. Ice, cracking like a tired back as she lowered the glass down. A sharp, fizzy sensation as the alcohol turned into curiosity. Stubbing her cigarette out, she took herself back inside.

After a laboured whir her inbox reappeared. She clicked on the subject line and read.

Dear Susan,

I hope you don't mind me emailing you out of the blue like this. My name is Nicola Long, Michelle Long's daughter.

A tiny kernel of lime burst against Susan's back tooth. She tried to put a face to the name but failed.

I've been working with the letters you donated to the Feminist Assembly. During my time in the archive they have come to be very important to me, and I feel I've grown very close to the woman who wrote them. I'm an artist myself and I understand many of the struggles that she faced in her lifetime, I think I'm not mistaken in saying that lots of young women would. I'd like to propose that an exhibition be held, both of her pots and her letters together. I've been in touch with Clementine Moreau at Endo Works gallery, London, who is interested in the project, and there has been talk of the possibility of a publication.

Susan pushed her gin and tonic to outside her line of vision, obscured by the gangly leaves of a spider plant. Its insistent bubbles were somehow too like the voice glowing at her from the screen. A voice she did not want in her mouth. The voice ran on regardless.

I feel that because of my deep connection with her, I would be able to bring her back to life in this way with insight and sensitivity, but there are a few things that don't make sense to me. I'm curious to know why—

Susan's shoulders wrung the top of her spine like a rag. The nerve of it was almost laughable. Poor – her eyes scanned back to the top – Nicola, who seemed to think that life was hers to make sense of, that anything was.

Then the punchline:

Fate.

What an ability, Susan thought. To be able to live one's life like that, as if it were an opera! She had to laugh now, and she did. Well, Nicola, as she reached for her drink from between the leaves and took a gulp, choking to death at thirty-three? There was no sense! That's what she would tell her, if she were to tell her anything. She'd read the letters hadn't she, and was that not proof enough? If it wasn't, God help us all.

She clicked the small x in the left-hand corner of the screen and the email disappeared. Condensation covered her glass. She picked it up and carried it outside to catch the last few hours of sun, which was warm for early spring. It folded over her from between the houses, fluttering with its low shadow as her feet pressed into the grass from where she sat on the edge of the decking. She brought her knees up to her chin and wrapped her arms around them. The almond smell of her moisturiser mixed with sweat and the faint depth of wet soil.

33

'Morning.'

Marcella stood up, to show she wanted more than a good morning.

'Susan called yesterday evening. She's asked for the letters to be removed from the archive and returned to her.' Nicola was standing in front of her, fiddling with her lip, as Marcella scanned her eyes for recognition. 'But it sounds like you managed to track her down, so maybe you know this already?'

'I didn't track her down, I *know* her.'

'She mentioned this. I think what's happened, as far as I understand, is that she feels too much time has passed and she doesn't want to reopen old wounds. It's very personal, this material. We have to be respectful of that.'

'Reopen?' interrupted the coarse parrot of Nicola's voice. 'But it's a *public* archive. They were always—'

'I'm just as much in the dark as you are about all of this, but they belong to her, and she has the right to remove them if she wants to.'

'But I haven't finished reading them. I was going to do an exhibition with her, did she tell you? I'm sure she'd want that, for her friend. She must have misunderstood, that's all. Can't you call her back and explain?'

'She made it very clear that her decision was final. I've arranged for a courier to bring everything back to her this week. If you want to chase her up on it, you'd be doing so without my blessing. Speaking on behalf of the archive, I have to respect her privacy. We have to respect her privacy.'

Nicola turned into her mother then, Well I Never! and visibly baulked. Privacy?

A TV churned with laughter.

'God, she's so *fat*,' breathed Aimee Zhang as Jade Goody wriggled into the hot-red creases of her nakedness, live on the screen. Then, 'I'm starving. Let's make Pop Tarts!'

Nicola, aged thirteen, stood up in agreement. A small, very dark circle of blood marked where she'd been sitting on the settee.

'Ergh, Nic. Look.' Aimee turned up the volume and dug her chipped purple nail polish into the upholstery, twitching. 'Well do something, *quick!*'

In the unknown territory of the Zhangs' kitchen, Nicola rummaged under the sink. She returned to the living room with a dish sponge and a cereal bowl full of water and washing up liquid. 'Hurry *up*,' Aimee hissed. 'If my mum sees this she'll fucking kill me. So *fucking* gross. *Quickly!*'

'Don't tell anyone about this,' pleaded Nicola as she forced the fabric under the sponge, seeping pink suds.

The following Monday a reconstruction of the scene spread like spilt honey through the greased-up corridors of their comprehensive school, clinging to the fissured ceiling and coating the nascent lip hair of boys. 'Apparently,' they whispered through mouths flecked with monster munch and sticky with the sweets of her innards, 'it stank!'

The reek of her crotch was only to be surpassed when two days later, copying the structure of a cell into a lined exercise book, Caileigh Summer's tiny moans had played out from a Motorola speaker. Her small voice quivering with false, practised passion. The silence of Double Science aroused into a flame. Caileigh's boyfriend Daniel, holding the phone open on the table, had recorded her the previous afternoon. The class screeched their metal stools around to face the sound, not in outrage but in awe. Privacy died the second Becca King spat out the pen lid she'd been chewing to shout Play it again, and the class, in unison, cried Yes!

'I'm sorry, I know you've spent a lot of time with them.'

'I thought that's why she was put here. I don't understand why she wouldn't want it.'

'Whatever her reasoning,' Marcella offered, before repeating herself for what she hoped would be the final time: 'We have to respect her wishes. It's the right thing to do.' Her posters hung behind her, reinforcing the point. It's the right thing to do, they chanted in block capital letters, fists in the air. Nicola gripped the table's edge. Everything was disappearing, the way it always did. She watched as the word Renaissance, still bobbing above her, slowly lost its gold-green shimmer until a child poked a finger through the floating R and the whole thing deflated. The child holding the bubble kit that was her life; the one who was using it wrong.

'Thank you for being so understanding,' said Marcella, touching Nicola's shoulder gently with the tips of her fingers. 'Don't be a stranger. We're having a fundraiser next Tuesday at four, Jenny is making vegan cupcakes. Perhaps you could bring something?'

Nicola repeated Cupcakes and Tuesday and showed her teeth. 'I'll try,' she said, swallowing the child down inside her.

In the stairwell of Poseidon House the strip lights flickered and clicked. At the bottom of the echoing flight, two doors: one led to the linoleum-clad foyer, the other, out into a backstreet with bins and puddles. EMERGENCY EXIT ONLY, printed in vinyl on the door's mottled glass. Underneath, across the metal of its armature: PUSH TO OPEN – ALARM WILL SOUND. I want you to be happy, I want you to know how.

You dip the wand in the liquid, take it out carefully and blow. No, not like that. That's too fast. No, you're holding it too tight. If you tilt it, it will spill. No, not on the carpet. You have to blow outwards, like this. Not in your mouth, please, don't eat it, not rough like that, not upside down or in your eye, not with two hands, it will fall. No, you're not listening. You are doing it wrong, you are using it wrong. Stop.

The child she'd swallowed fell to all fours. It was banging on the floor of her with feet and fists. There is no right way, it screamed. Otherwise why would you give it to *me?*

Nicola pushed on the fire doors with both hands flat.

The sharp screech of a bell rang out. It tore through the concrete stairwell before ripping into the main building, banging against the plasterboard and loosening the ceiling panels. Nicola stood very still. Throughout Poseidon House people stolidly cleaned their paint brushes, tapped their keyboards, scratched their noses and ignored it, the sound, though it kept on regardless, like a madman, catastrophizing only for himself. Someone coughed very quietly, as if to shame him for his indiscretion, but he wouldn't stop. Save your souls, he shouted, Fire! Unable to continue their tasks in the presence of this lunatic any longer, the building's inhabitants began to humour him; reluctantly, laptops closed, rucksacks were half zipped and slung over one shoulder, jackets went on but weren't buttoned. Everyone slowly stood up. In the act of unexpectedly moving as one, the crowd suddenly stampeded. They pushed past Nicola and the door she had opened to assemble in the alleyway, where, facing an afternoon now irretrievably disrupted, rucksacks committed to a second shoulder and jackets closed up in defeat.

Only Nicola remained.

The dust and the cobwebs on the staircase walls, dislodged by the backs of the building's former occupants, circled anew to the sound of a bell. She watched them dancing in the wrong direction. The riches of passing things, they sang, are as an unfaithful guest.

197

It would not be stealing, she reasoned, as she wove her way back to the place she'd been banished from. Not really. Merely borrowing. She would simply finish what she had started, and bring them back. No one would miss them. It would only be a small detour, a very minor delay.

Rustled by the unexpected flight, the Feminist Assembly felt strangely unfamiliar as she stepped back in. It was as though she'd opened the door to find on the other side not a Special Collection, cocooned in silk, but the back end of a stage taped with floor markings and thin plywood buttresses for the walls; a shoddy appendage to the facade. No one flinched, or frowned, or peered over their glasses with a finger to their lips. No one was here, only over-stuffed cardboard boxes, stacks of pink manila wallets, their dye lost in gradations to the sun, flyers and posters and notices for events long past: everything piled up and peeling, like the neglected rooms of a crank. She pondered how much authority silence had. Without it, even the inanimate lapsed. Pages from an open book fanned in the breeze. Then, with the drama of lights dimming before a performance, the alarm very suddenly stopped.

This time, the silence came back with an edge.

How long did she have? She hurried over to the booth she'd just minutes ago been told to leave, the box of letters still lying in its flat wooden arms. She moved quickly, increasingly aware of the mercurial stage set in front of her as the orchestra in her lower intestine assembled their instruments.

Boo.

Her father appeared over the top of the reading booth's wooden frame. He was gesticulating wildly, with a rolled-up newspaper supplement in one hand and a glass of wine in the other, his red breath booming: In future, Nicola, if you can't use something properly, you won't get to use it at all. Her mother, fussing behind him with a potato peeler, bustled forward to join in. I know, silly woman. She took a deep breath and strode towards them. Her mother disappeared in a starchy white plume but her father remained, shrouded in darkness now and sitting at a dining room table, his glass of wine set down at his side. A Christmas tree blinked in the background, illuminating his furrowed brow as he bent his whole body over a mermaid's Lego palace in utter, selfish, concentration. The palace that when Nicola woke up on Christmas morning she found already assembled on her behalf, after ripping open the wrapping of its empty, feather-light box. In future, if you can't use something properly . . . he muttered into the night as he placed one Lego block on top of the other, pausing only to top up his glass. The orchestra adjusted their sheet music. The conductor rose to his feet. In future. No. She pushed against the swipe of the conductor's hand, which swirled with a flourish into the nothingness of her father's glass, and grasped the box she wasn't allowed to have. This one, this time, had weight. She exhaled into the unexpected struggle of it, before adjusting her posture to shift the centre and forcing her breath towards the door. After a harried manoeuvre involving elbows, shoulders, hipbones and ankles – the brief assistance of her left temple, twisted neck – she managed to open it and was out. Out into the cold draughty stairwell and down the steps. Not through the fire escape into the backstreets with the rest of the evacuees, scrolling through their phones and waiting for instructions, but into the foyer and out the front door. Out into the anonymous rush of Southwark Street at lunchtime: briefcases, pushchairs and worried women running. Knock, knock, knock. That's the way to do it!

It was not stealing, she repeated to herself as the black cab approached the kerb and she opened the sliding door, heaved the box onto its non-slip rubber floor, and buckled her seatbelt. Going through with it! She didn't even care how high the meter ran in comparison to an Uber. This taxi had passed with the timing of a getaway car, and the driver deserved every scaling increment of twenty-pence pieces he could get.

It was not stealing. She noticed fresh scuffs on the box's four bottom corners as they drove away. The dent in its side. It was not.

Kicking aside a tattered pair of bamboo slippers and an empty can of tuna with a fork in it, she squeezed her way into her bedroom; it sat at the top of a townhouse in the converted attic of converted flats. Her single bed took up most of the cramped space. On the windowsill lay the modest tableau of a rose quartz crystal, an empty champagne bottle, a rabbit's foot keyring and a vase, glazed in an overrun peach brown and holding a few sprigs of dried thistle, all under a thin film of dust. A snow globe with the Eiffel tower in it, a little less dusty.

Nicola dropped her cargo onto the bed and crawled across the scrunched-up sheets to join it as the door clicked shut behind her. The weathered receipt she'd been using to mark her place had slipped down and out of sight during the journey, but it didn't matter. She knew exactly where she was: she was near the end. She moved her fingers greedily through to find the last French postmark and tugged the envelope that followed it out. The stationery it was written on, with its pastel twists of wildflowers, looked immediately at home in her room, surrounded by the blossomy bruise of car-boot sale trinkets. More than it had ever done in the Feminist Assembly. Whatever song of vandalism and disorder the orchestra in her lower gut had been warming up to play was instantly forgotten. No one, she thought, could look at these letters in this room and call it theft. They belonged here.

Well, here we are. It would seem I have returned, back to square one.

The kettle whistles and Donna shifts from her seat to silence it, its screech accompanied by a hiss of hot steam; the smell of mildew, exhaust fumes and pink soap hanging on its breath. In the flat above, an onion cooks. As she pours the water from the kettle, the radio reports on a fire the previous night: there is reason to believe it was caused by a lit match discarded on a wooden escalator. She blows on her knuckles and prods at the teabag with a knife. Dark brown flames circle the silver in an underwater reconstruction of the blaze, before being extinguished by a glug of milk.

After Donna left for France, Leonie rented her room to a young Spanish woman who was now pregnant, and it wouldn't be fair to uproot her, not now, Leonie had said when she'd asked for it back. She'd been on the verge of returning to her mother in Basford when Harry had swooped in at the last minute to offer his recently deceased aunt's flat: a neglected basement in Bethnal Green, with a long and narrow private garden. She wipes the sleeve of her dressing gown on the window to reveal where, in the thicket of overgrown branches and stone bird baths, the colour green still wrestles somewhere under the frost.

Living off the handouts of others again it would seem, but at least I'm back in the city, so somewhat more cosmopolitan if less idyllic. The flat is very strange – I'm sure you'll see it soon enough but I'll describe it anyway. Big and old-fashioned, sort of how I imagine a 1920s hotel or an ocean liner to be. Well, maybe not an ocean liner – all the furniture is on wheels! But you know what I mean. Lots of wood and gilt and heaviness. That being said, if you leave the connecting doors propped open the light runs the whole way through from the garden to the street side.

My sudden ejection back into (almost) homelessness and definite joblessness has not been pleasant I must say. The first few weeks back were mainly just crying and carrying on, I'm ashamed to admit, which is why this letter is so late. I wish I had a magic 8-ball I could shake, something that would tell me in no uncertain terms what was coming next. I feel completely beset by it all, that age-old worry of whether or not you will ever get it right, if anyone ever has? Anyway, what was I doing? Describing. So! Two big rooms in a line and a long garden and lots of light, despite being six feet beneath the pavement. All in all, fairly dated and downtrodden but it has a sort of faded glamour which I like, of course.

I'm yet to unpack, you'll be shocked to hear. All my belongings are just sitting about in piles. I know I'd feel more settled if I did but something tells me not to get too comfortable, possibly history. Well. Don't pity me. I really do feel much more composed and in control after my brief spell away. It has given me the gift of realisation: namely, that London stinks and I shouldn't ever take it too seriously. The whole scene is rigged and the only thing for it is to stop looking over my shoulder at everyone else and keep my nose to the grindstone. It's the only way to take things. No one else can do it in my place. You know, I thought that leaving France was such a big crash, but what I've learnt is that these crashes are part of an inescapable cycle: Life! Work hard, fall down, despair, take a look around, get back up again. When Dev went and left me all alone in a pissing field I thought I would just drop down dead, but I didn't! And at least I can recognise and acknowledge these shifts for what they are now, which seems to be a breakthrough. It takes so much energy to keep beginning new lives but I am resolved to try. To be more aware of my surroundings and accept change with ease and an open mind. And besides, I still have enough strength to climb out of the drain a few more times yet!

Now, the good news. Please read slowly as there isn't much. In a few weeks I will be starting as an assistant technician at the City of London Polytechnic for the adult

203

*evening classes. It will only be things like showing people
how to wedge clay and clearing up after lessons etc, but I
reckon there'll be the chance to do a bit of teaching if I play
my cards right and behave. Most importantly, I will get to
use the workshop after hours. Joe etc sold the old arch whilst
I was away and now they've all got studios of their own up
and running. I, on the other hand, haven't made anything
since I got back. Truth be told I feel a little afraid to. I feel
afraid to make the kind of things I was making in France.
Jan was so non-judgemental, and it's a whole different ball
game keeping those kinds of experiments up in the tiger's
mouth. But, I suppose, being after hours and all, no one
will see, so I'll have some time to get back into the swing of
things without having to produce any masterpieces on the
spot.*

*What else? I am going to be a bridesmaid next June. You
remember Rose? From Stoke? Well it's her wedding in
Manchester. I know, I'm no longer the spring chicken I was
at yours but hey ho. I've been putting boiled lemon juice in
my hair.*

Nicola lay on her side with one arm dangling off the bed.
The other held her reading material close to her face,
crumpling the paper from the centre. Occasionally she
heard her phone vibrate in her bag but ignored it.
Whatever it was, it didn't seem urgent. After the thrill of
her escape nothing did. The whole afternoon felt as
though it had been sedated; the laziness that comes with
early spring and unexpected time, like an empty bucket
rolling.

Without anyone to keep an eye on her, she no longer went to the trouble of putting each letter back in its envelope, then back in its box. Instead she dropped each page to one side when it was done. They fell to the floor, floating down into a pile. Their words filled the room, seeping under crusted deodorant caps and into half-empty glasses of water, settling on the tacky rubber bed of an eyelash curler, giving everything that belonged to her the cast of their mooning, *my flower*, the colour of dust.

I feel I am all determination and no potential. Organising boring shitty things and generally pushing. Worrying a lot. That old slog. It's impossible not to fall back on old habits. I can't shake the feeling that I am stuck in time, or have been catapulted back through it somehow. Everyone else seems to always be moving in different directions, and I suppose I am too, but it feels more like a spiral than an upward hike. On and on, round and round. For all my gloom all my love is just existing and counting the days. Trying to find some routine or purpose. It seems like only months ago that I was working so hard and producing so much, and now nothing? My fear is that I have gone and trod too lightly through the world and now I have so little to hold on to. Only tomorrow. Tomorrow and tomorrow and tomorrow and the day after that. Tomorrow is all over everything, always rearing its ugly head just when I think I've gone and got it, like a mole with a hammer. And let me tell you, there is nothing like waking with a sore head to remind you how fleeting the feeling is, just last night I was swimming: gallons of lager, total happiness after seeing Joe, then complete memory loss, snapped heel, told off. A rather grinding autobiography, isn't it? Same old, same old, but it can't be helped. Life, when it is happening, doesn't care to tell you which part is telling and what it tells. That is the frustration. I suppose all this aimless rambling is caught up in feelings of pointlessness and futility and the ever-increasing sense of ageing into an absence where every addition feels like a load, wiping tables, wedging clay. I must say, I do enjoy being in the college after hours, toiling away in private. It's a little bit like gardening, or masturbating. Secret, under the soil, and I do know and trust that eventually I'll get my rhythm back. A little bit of mindlessness never hurt anyone, but it does have its pains. And there is guilt, of course. Of course there is guilt.

Excuse me. The postman seems to be leering through the window. So impatient. Well at least I'm not the only one. And would you look at that? He brings a little cattle prod to jab me with: Leonie's big writeup in the Ceramic Review. I do wonder why I am so ignored by any kind of establishment. I know there is no fairness in the world, but looking back it does seem I've been subjected to an unfortunate number of near misses. A kind of disregard verging on the conspiratorial, don't you agree? As if someone, somewhere, is armed with a doll and a pin. This erratic handwriting is only because I've got my overcoat on and am freezing to death. Honestly, I don't know how Harry's aunt survived here. Well, I suppose she didn't, did she? Oh dear! No but we shouldn't joke, poor darling, all alone here underground. Perhaps I should get on the phone to Harry and find out what it was that finished her off, because if it was the cold I fear I won't fare much better! God, it is miserable though.

Jumper on top of jumper on top of jumper. Always trying to get on with it. And I am: pruned back some of the branches in the garden and swept all the dead leaves and I must say it has potential. I will have to talk to Harry about how much I'm able to interfere, so to speak, but the place is so overgrown I doubt he'd care much. I'd love to chop down the ragged old willow at the back. I'm fairly certain it's diseased and the light that would come in its place would be spectacular I think.

One page and then another. It was like the games Nicola had played as a child, folding paper into a pyramid with an open middle.

Pick a number? Count.

Pick a colour? Spell it out.

In the centre, nearly worn to a hole by the curious fingers of little girls, is where the answer, on an axis, revolved. In and out and open, in and out and open, this is how it ends.

A stroke! He says it was a stroke that killed her! So apparently there's hope for me yet.

Her phone kept ringing. Nicola lifted her head from the pillow and wiped something from her eye. A miniature sea urchin of black gunk glistened at her from her fingertip. She wiped it on the sheets and dragged her bag across the floor towards her without getting up. Six missed calls. She wondered if it'd be Marcella Goodwoman herself on the other end, or if the matter would have been escalated to someone more severe. Security, perhaps? She paused for a moment to consider what kind of security an archive might have, and what punishments such a force might employ. Through the gap in the curtains the sky had changed to a deep, unspoilt ultramarine; it was twilight, and the archive would be closing soon. She turned off her phone and shoved it under the mattress.

Bah Humbug. Danced around Harrods for a little while to try and get into the spirit of things but it didn't do much good. There is something very melancholic about decorating the shortening days in tinsel. Saw Marcus for a coffee in Soho. Ian's flat in Chinatown and all his things have gone to his first wife from a hundred years ago, and there's nothing he can do about it. He didn't seem himself at all, very tired with huge bags under his eyes, and he snapped a lot. Told me off for playing with the toggles on my coat. He says he's going to live in France and see out old age with Jan, which made me feel very sad. I can't explain it but something about meeting him and Ian felt like part of a new chapter for me, like life was really starting to open up and make sense and now it has all fallen apart so quickly and changed beyond recognition, like it never even happened. Selfish, I know, to always be thinking about people in terms of what they mean to me, but it's the reality of how I feel and if I can't tell you then who can I tell?

The college has broken up for Christmas and truth be told I don't think I'm going back. In the end it was far worse than even my most humble expectations. Pushing trolleys of appalling hobbyist crap – sugar bowls for Mother's Day, etc,

etc – down dark corridors at night. Scrubbing tables, sweeping up. It dawned on me soon enough that it was just a glorified cleaning job. Like I said, back to square one. The hours gave my days an awful pattern too. Pacing around the freezing flat all day only to then go and pace through empty halls. So of course I'm out the door . . . but I must ask, is this a flaw I have, do you think? To always be looking for something else, something better? Or is it a strength? I suppose that all hinges on luck, doesn't it. If I succeed it's the later, if not, then well it's not. But really, how else could a person live? Surely a person has to always be looking for the next thing, the better thing? Onwards and upwards as it were. Or is this mindset simply proof that I've absorbed the dreaded mantra of our iron führer?

Susan, tell me, what have I made for myself?

You seem to move very seamlessly from one thing to the next without falling into swamps of childish deliberation and growing pains. Life, for you, seems to move very naturally in the right direction. But then again you've always been like that, you've always had a very zen-like contentment with your lot, whereas I've always been so hungry for more.

Her handwriting curled into the margins and tacked itself to the vines, the girlish loops going blue in the face as they ran to the edges. Caught in a twist of Queen Anne's lace was a small transparent stain, overlooked by Nicola who'd already dropped the page onto the pile at her bedside and reached for the next. Susan, reading first and still holding onto it, pauses to wipe a smear of custard off her daughter's face as she runs past, banging a drum on a string around her neck. Patience thinning, she calls after her to be quiet.

But then again you've always been like that, still ringing in her ears.

The drum string breaks and for a brief and gorgeous moment the noise abates, before becoming a clatter, gasps and then tears. Susan puts down the letter and lifts Jenna up.

'Mummy fix it.'

Fine. She takes the knot and reties it. Heart hardened by the comment that forbade her any complaint, she wipes the custard from her thumb onto the letter at her side, smudging it purposefully, a protest: I have hungers too! Their evidence, now, a small stain face down on a stranger's carpet, blotting her out anew.

Above them Nicola's eyes were tiring. She let her lids close and brought her hands up to her cheeks. Making her whole body follow the line of her neck she did a long little lizard stretch and then stepped out of bed. The floorboards funnelled a draught between her toes, good morning! With a toothbrush clenched between her teeth she rushed to pull on socks and wrestle with the hard metal buttons of her jeans; she was late for something but didn't know what. The minutes were passing quicker than usual. It had been spring before, but now it was dark. She tries to hurry to the station, but her shoe chafes the back of her ankle. She shouldn't have worn these, she thinks, knows, they do not fit. She increases her speed and feels the skin of her heel begin to tear. When she reaches the platform it's already Thursday. A train pulls in, a blister forms and then pops.

The paper on the seat beside her shows faces she doesn't recognise beneath words that haven't changed: No Concessions, In We Go, Count the Loss. Blood from her heel is making itself permanent on the leather, the leather gnaws at the bone. She feels the cold, the air pressure, the years. Her eyes feel clogged with dust. Her mouth feels clogged with dust. The windows too. Spitting on her hands she clears the dust from her eyes and the windows. Outside an old woman is running alongside the tracks. She is wearing a swimming costume and has a swimming cap on her head. She is running as fast as the train. As she keeps pace she whips herself with a sunflower. Water and yellow petals trail behind her. *Why don't you come and join me on the other side?* she calls as she hurls herself forwards. Gases rising off her like steam: all of her cells coming out of the way, swirling behind her in plumes. She keeps on running but there is less and less of her. No costume anymore, just nylon threads, seams, eyelashes, cotton fibres, shadows, bones. Everything falling and falling to the ground, until only her hands and mouth are chasing the train – flying beside it – suspended in the wind. *The sun is out over here!* the mouth shouts. A single finger curls: *Come.*

When Nicola woke the room was cool and quiet and between her breasts the skin was damp. Outside, streetlights clicked on one by one. Creeping across a neighbour's roof, a fox caught a gutter on its back leg and the rustle of the world whispered itself back in. Reaching under the mattress she felt around for her phone and turned it on: eight thirty. She downed the stale centimetre of water in her glass and got up, for real this time, although the feeling, eyes clogged with dust, mouth clogged with dust, remained. Creaking, she carried herself through the empty flat towards the kitchen. There were only a few letters left, she could probably finish them tonight. But first, first she would need a coffee. The feeling in her right hand had been lost to sleep; she stood, making a fist and then stretching it out again to bring sensation back, while the gas warmed the water inside the percolator. As she watched the blue flame, the reality of what she'd done that afternoon, which was beginning to seem more and more like a theft, slowly shifted into something resembling guilt; it seemed clear to her now that what lay on her bed was not a pile of papers, but a person.

What if that person rolled over? Parted the hair at the back of their head, and showed the woodlice writhing beneath.

True to its nature, guilt twisted into fear.

The coffee pot bubbled. She turned off the gas and splashed her face in the sink. Don't be mad. It was Susan who'd abandoned her, Susan who'd left her boxed up all alone, starved of oxygen in the dark with no reply. Susan, Nicola testified to the empty room, who didn't want to bring her back. If anyone should be afraid of her, it was Susan. Susan didn't understand her, *she* did. Going back upstairs she turned the hall light on, just in case.

34

Her long hair brushes over her hand as she pats the chair beside her. 'Now it's your turn.'

'Marion just read my Tarot cards,' says Leonie, holding the vacant chair by its back, 'They said . . . what did they say, Marion? Tell her.'

'The Sun, the Star, the Nine of Cups, and the Ace of Pentacles. Wealth and gifts and triumph.'

'The world!' Leonie makes a circle with her hands like a backing singer as she says it, before adding an urgent '*Well*,' and rattling the chair back and forth on the floorboards: 'Don't you want to know?'

'Knock the deck with your knuckles as you ask it a question,' Marion instructs.

'Do I have to say it aloud?'

'It would help, but no, not if you don't want to.'

Donna knocks and keeps silent. Behind their heads a pile of records falls to the ground, fanning out across the rug. Two men, both bearded, argue about the music. Record sleeves are brandished and fingers are pointed, accusations of misinterpreting the mood. Marion continues to shuffle the cards as the party around her escalates. Unfazed as a crowd of new arrivals storms into the room, ring pulls hissing and vinyl cracking underfoot. She starts to deal. The Two of Swords appears first, upside down. Leonie makes a noise with the back of her throat. 'I don't like the look of that blindfold.'

'*Shhhh.*'

Death comes above it, backwards. Marion takes a cracker from the bowl beside her and starts to crunch, small crumbs falling into the cavern between her breasts. Donna watches with disgust, already against her. Justice. Van Morrison wins the war behind their backs. 'Queen of the Slipstream', crooning through the smoke-filled flat. The Chariot and the King of Wands are laid down now, both reversed, making the pyramid on the table complete.

'*Ah,*' says Marion, shaking her head. 'You are very stubborn. Too stubborn, perhaps. Stuck in a stalemate. It will take work to change your path. Yes. Mills and wheels. An inner purging.' As she speaks her fingers wind an invisible thread. Donna sucks in her cheeks.

'Thank you, *Marion,*' she says, draining her glass and walking off into a kitchen filled with people. They are leaning on the worktops and each other.

'I want a bump of something,' she demands of the sprawl.

'I hear the Tarot forebodes?' says Joseph, lifting a key of white powder to her nose. He runs his fingers up her ribs and makes the noise of a ghost with his mouth in an O.

'Oh fuck off,' pushing her way through to the garden toward the first person she sees with a cigarette in their mouth.

'Can I bum one?'

A man with a pilling red jumper and a thick black moustache offers her the packet and his name, John.

'How do you know Leonie?' lighting her up.

'I used to live here.'

'You a potter as well?'

Her pupils are pooling.

'No.'

'What do you do?'

'Oh, nothing much.'

She smiles sweetly as she says it, dipping her shoulders like she used to do with the men at the restaurant, a chemical taste cascading down her throat. *Nothing, I do nothing,* leaning against the edge of a brick barbeque, blowing smoke and watching the mouths of strangers move. A bonfire crackles and pops at their side, tongues of fluttering orange bat the edges of her vision, stinking of car tyres. Her mind goes to her pots in France, they appear to her like the air from her lungs, twisting out into the darkness, independent of her. Of anyone. Like scarecrows left in a field. Fluttering only slightly on the horizon line, smashed and reassembled. Deaf and blind and silent, scattered here and there in shards. It makes her heart feel tired to think of them, out there. The sheer mass of what she has made and left. She slides down to rest with her hands on her knees, her tired heart thumping a little too fast. She wishes this John person would take his hand off her shoulder and shut up for a second, but he keeps on chattering like a tin can. His face has a heat inside it that is starting to flicker near the surface, worse and worse as he speaks. She looks up, around, everyone does. It makes their skin seem less and less solid, so that it frightens her.

She thinks of Susan, nine years old and crouching in her father's garden shed, hidden among the wood saws and the tins of paint. He'd denied them dinner the previous evening for some long-forgotten crime, and they were still reeling from the injustice. In a rare act of vengeance Susan took the gum from her mouth and put it in the jaws of her father's bench vice. 'Watch this,' she said as she wound it tight, the gum bulging like a baby's arm and reeking of watermelon and sawdust. Then she span the steel handle back on itself, stringing the pink stuff out into a scream. That's what all their faces look like, flickering in the garden. There is nothing robust or good about them anymore.

'I was born in the Royal Free and I'll die in the Royal Free,' someone announces through the flames. Donna turns her head to the source. A woman is swinging on a wooden swing strung up on a tree branch, the wine in her coupe glass swishing like storm waves. 'What can I say, I'm a woman of NW3,' she sings. The words kick Donna right in the back. She feels certain she's never disliked anyone more, she has never hated anyone more than this woman who can predict where she will end up dead, as simply as if she were stating the date.

She pushes herself off the brickwork and stumbles back inside. Leonie catches her in the doorframe, reeling, 'Marion's having a *vision*, it's fabulous.' Behind her wibbling head Joseph is sitting on a sofa with his arms stretched out across its top, he is talking to a woman perched on the coffee table in front. He is smiling with his whole face, then he is touching hers.

I suppose the problem, or part of it, has been my moving around so much. Abandoning Stoke for the hopes of something better in London. Then off to France and now back again. I haven't had a chance to really settle anywhere, to find my footing and let my work ease into its own. I've seen glimmers of what it could be, of course, and felt I was getting close at points, but something always creeps up and forces me back to the beginning again. That pain I spoke of before, of always having to start new lives. I can't lie and say I am not exhausted by it.

You will laugh and think I'm being over-sensitive, but Leonie's party, I don't even know how to explain it. It felt like being caught by a wave when you're swimming. Like the world has an order I'll never be able to change – like I wasn't even there. I guess I have always felt a little like an outsider and known that my path would be a different one, but somehow having my fortune told or whatever you call it, and seeing Joe with that girl and maybe also being back in the old house and missing it a little, and then coming back here to where I'm so alone. Being older too, of course.

I wonder why I ever took up pottery in the first place. It hurts me to have these images in my head, this ideal of how I want my work to be, only to find I can never fully realise it. To open the kiln door and find cracks and explosions, or worse: plain old disappointment. It is the constant disappointment that makes me think I should just give it up. But, by some strange compulsion, I seem to carry on. It's like how they say that after childbirth you forget the pain of it, so as to keep going. Some version of that must be true of art, too. Because even after all the hurt and frustrations I seem to find myself back at it. That rush of closing the kiln door to the unknown, and dreaming of what might meet me on the other side. How marvellous everything could potentially turn out, and how you might finally catch it, the image. Though of course you never do.

It's almost addictive, that feeling. It is a kind of optimism, I think, as I have said before, and for that reason I am not deterred. This morning I woke up full of foreboding, probably unhelped by Marion and her idiotic predictions. Mills and wheels, really. Nonetheless, awful thoughts like I wish I could just put a line through everything and start again, and in some ways I do, I do wish I could just start again . . . It is my strongest wish. Well, anyway, before any of this could take a real hold I noticed that the bulbs I planted in the garden when I moved in have tiny buds at the end of their shoots. They'll probably flower any day now.

So, life goes on! While I've been busy moaning to you about the college and the freezing cold, winter was quietly seeing itself off, and, lo and behold, it seems to have gone. Soon the days will be longer and the sun will come out and I'll have a garden full of daffodils. This is all to say that the wish to start again is already happening, it is the order of the seasons. I just need to buck up and meet it.

What else? Some especially fun gossip is that Harry – who you met at my birthday – is now dating an actress from Eastenders, *of all things. I won't tell you who because I want you to guess. It is not the obvious choice!*

Answers on the back of a postcard please.
Love,
xxx

The sound of a neighbour clearing their throat travelled through the walls. Nicola ran her tongue along her teeth. Reading had forced a film to form in her mouth. She sat inside it, looking out from her head at the darkened room, stewing in the space that finishing makes. A vacant feeling filling the air, like so much purple fog.

After her bladder had emptied itself she sat on the toilet staring at the wall for a very long time. From within the contours of plaster, paint and shadow, a dog stared back at her. Silent and searching, with one black spot circling his left eye. He tilted his head towards her in the darkness as if to speak before an ambulance drove past, its blue siren intruding through the bathroom's opaque glass, and he broke apart. She heard a key turn in the lock downstairs, then footsteps. Her flatmate must be back, rattling around as he always did, soaking beans and washing his clothes too often. Nicola didn't want to see him. She no longer wanted to be there, in her house, her home, the bardo. Still sitting on the toilet in the dark, she took her phone down from the window ledge to find an alternative. It was Friday, after all.

At the pub Alice and Jason were sitting in a booth, huddled around a single phone. Neither looked up when Nicola slid along the other side of the wooden bench. Their eyes, fixed intently on the screen between them, were sparkling like bird scarers. It was late in the evening and the pub around them had descended into disorder. Tables and chairs had been moved from where they usually stood to accommodate groups of people in shifting sizes and the empty glasses were piling up, giving the space a weedy, cavernous feeling.

'I need to see that again,' said Jason. Alice moved her thumb and they both watched as what was gripped in her fingers replayed, before letting out a shared shriek and finally looking up. 'Nicola, you're going to *love* this.'

'Look at what *Lily Topher* just posted.'

'She's so fucking mentally *ill*.'

'Let me see properly,' Nicola said, leaning forwards. Alice relinquished her phone, handing it across the table so she could get a better look. In her palm Lily Topher danced nude in front of a full-length mirror, with an emoji covering her crotch. The chick one, emerging from its egg. It was not an exuberant dance, or a long one, just a slow little wriggle that repeated like a glitch. She'd posted four in the space of an hour. According to the table, an obvious sign of disarray. Nicola observed the scandal distractedly. She did not love it as much as they'd expected, though she had been mildly interested to see that Lily Topher, underneath her clothes, was not as toned as one would think. What Nicola wanted was to talk about her day. She wanted to tell her friends about taking the letters and reaching their end. Only something was keeping her outside of herself, that purple fog she'd felt descending in her room. It was not an unfamiliar sensation, and after a moment she was able to place it. It was the experience she sometimes had leaving the cinema after going alone. The film had temporarily removed her from her life, and now that she had been returned to it she would have to readjust, retune her hearing, blink. Only the film was part of her life now as well. Readjusting would involve recalibrating the two. And for that short while neither her life nor the film seemed entirely real. That was it, she thought. That fog. That was it?

It was so mundane.

'There's more,' said Alice, snatching the phone back. 'Let me find them.'

As Alice searched, more people appeared at the booth, squeezing themselves in along the bench. She waved one hand in vague introduction, while the other continued to scroll. Somebody suggested shots.

Nicola opened her bedroom door at one a.m. to find the letters still strewn across her bed and floor. As she edged through the tiny room they moved slowly about her with their loops and their sighs, yellow and pink mixing with the vinegary product of cheap white wine and tequila on an empty stomach. Creeping vines. She began to gather them up.

She swept them in piles towards her chest with both arms and dropped them back into their box. They fell onto each other at jutted-out angles as she pushed them in with the flat of her hands. Their middles crumpling and their floral edges tearing as she forced them in to make space for more. One scoop of her arms and then another, pressing down.

How heavy does your head feel?

A wall of bowling balls falling.

Acid rose in her throat.

Marcella had lied!

The potter hadn't killed herself. She had planted daffodils.

She'd gone on and on: making plans and falling down and trying, always trying so terribly hard to live. She wasn't barricaded behind the steel wall of the sublime. She was *her*. And it was horrible.

With a hollow plastic clack the lid of the wheelie bin slammed shut, its sound echoing through the quiet street. Nicola wiped her hands on her thighs and let herself back into her flat to throw up.

35

'I don't know how to tell you this, but the Susan Baddeley Papers appear to have gone missing. I . . . you have to know that I'm so very embarrassed. Nothing like this has ever happened before. We have reason to believe it was Nicola Long who took them, but we've been unable to contact her. Guest passes only require a phone number, and, like I said, nothing like this has ever happened before. I can't tell you how sorry . . . You mentioned she tried to contact you? Would you be willing to follow that up? Of course we'd be happy to do it for you, if you passed on the email address. Really, Susan, anything. We're taking this matter very seriously . . .'

Susan pressed the red button to hang up.

'Who was that?' Jenna asked, handing her mother a paper plate carrying a large slice of pink birthday cake. She paused as she took it, wondering whether to tell.

Susan hadn't told her children, now both adults, about the letters, or the archive they were kept in. She'd always been a little afraid that, curious about the lives of their mothers before they existed, as children always are, they would be compelled to seek them out and read them. And she never could remember what about her they gave away, things she'd so far managed to keep apart from them. And besides, she was Bloom again now, not Baddeley. That person, whatever they would find of her between the lines, felt very far away.

But she had told them about Donna. She'd always felt it was her duty to. She'd told them that Donna was a person she'd known who was brave and strong and the equal of life itself, but who one day had let herself think otherwise. She had also told them that if they were ever nearing such a thought themselves, they should know that it was true of no one. Careful not to let complacency cloud her vigour, she sometimes thought she might have succeeded. It was a feeling that first struck her when someone asked about the pot. The pot that lived on the mantelpiece, that always got such compliments – to which her children always proudly responded that it had been made by a family friend who'd been an artist. A brilliant one. Even so, when she returns home from the birthday party she'll push it gently back on the mantelpiece as she passes, so that it stands a little more safely on its narrow perch, away from the edge.

'Oh, no one,' she said, setting her cake down on the grass beside her.

36

Joseph Birk lifts both his hands above his head before laying them on the shoulders of the elderly man who runs the bar, basically a kiosk, on the street leading back to his house. He kisses his forehead, much lower than his own, then leans on the counter to light a cigarillo. In only faintly accented Spanish he orders a shot of Hierbas and a beer, and assures the elderly man that Yes, yes, his father is still well, and Yes, of course, he will bring his friends back to have drinks before dinner. The blonde? smiles the old man. Yes, yes, he will bring the blonde. Then he throws his head back to down his shot. He stands, smoking at a leisurely pace, enjoying the familiar silence of his old friend, who is polishing a glass with a white cloth, and the way the air moves differently here under the heat: cura-tively hot, he thinks. It should be prescribed. Considering a second shot then thinking better of it he kisses the old man once more and walks back to join his guests at the house. Gloomy doorways hung with lace and plaited garlic line the steep street of ancient houses that make his way. Before going in, he leans against the windowsill of his own to tie his shoelace. Two floors above, on a balcony just big enough to sit on, is Donna. She sees his white tennis shoes glimmer and waves down, smiling, then hurries inside to meet him at the door. Bare feet slipping on the cool stone and hair still damp from the sea.

'We've been waiting for you. We were thinking we could grill the fish we bought this morning. Everyone's starving.'

He runs a hand through her hair to say Sure.

'Fuck!'

Harry booms from the kitchen, 'The fish have gone into bloody rigor mortis!' He is squatting in front of the fridge with both hands inside it, squeezing the cold fish bodies through the thin paper they'd been wrapped in and shaking his head. A cigar clenched firmly between his front teeth.

'We can't cook them until they're out of it.'

Without fish, their feast is flung into disarray. Boiled potatoes and grilled peppers seem odd by themselves and not at all luxurious, not holiday luxurious in any case. They riffle through the cupboards for additions. What if the cheese they were saving for afters gets baked in with the potatoes, like a kind of tartiflette? But that would be too heavy in this heat, they decide, as they pick their way through the options standing in the kitchen, smearing molten sheep's milk onto crackers, covering their bare toes in pale dust. In the absence of a consensus on the menu they open another bottle, which disappears in a breath between six. Then four bottles more. At midnight the potatoes are still sitting in a colander by the sink, scrubbed but not yet peeled.

Donna hums softly, blowing the cobwebs from a guitar and tuning the strings. Then filling the stone-walled rooms with her version of 'It Takes a Lot to Laugh, It Takes a Train to Cry'. Her audience, lying on the tiles with glasses of liquor balanced on their chests, spilling slightly with every laugh or breath, chimes in whenever she mis-remembers a line.

Break*man*, not break*down*.

Her voice is raspy and a little bit high and she back-tracks to correct herself, making the rendition slow and stilted, but with a sweetness that sustains the mood. Before falling asleep, red-faced and sticky, they raise a toast to the fish in the fridge:

'For resisting the grill!' they shout.

The following morning Donna wakes before everyone else. There'd been talk of taking a picnic down to the churchyard, and Joseph had boasted that the tomatoes here were the stuff of dreams.

I will go and buy them before everyone wakes up, she thinks. She's been waiting for an opportunity to go to the market on her own. It's her first trip abroad and she wants to take it all in properly, without Leonie and Harry bicker-ing behind her or Alison, Harry's girlfriend, catastrophising about the heat.

She steps out onto the orange cobbles and walks the polished incline towards the town centre, happiness swell-ing materially inside her. The streets, like birdsong, vibrate with the swell of morning; swinging the wicker basket at her side she smiles at her image in the eyes of the butcher, who gives her a wink. At the market, tomatoes are stacked in every direction: round and small and long and lumpy. Some with faces folded like old women who've lost their teeth, others with bright yellow skin. Yellow?

Shit. She so desperately wants to pick the right ones. She wants to return with her basket brimming and for Joseph to take her in his arms and say Hurrah! These are exactly right: the perfect tomatoes for our perfect lunch, making the holiday perfect.

But what if he says, What's this? Why have you brought me *these* tomatoes?

Before she can catch it happening, tears are streaming down her cheeks *and I was hiccupping with indecision. Blubbering like a baby, for God's sake!*

Well, to be more truthful, it was not indecision but fear. Fear that I would be outed as an ignoramus by my very knowledgeable and particular host. I don't know. I don't know why I'm always getting myself bent over backwards, ruining a perfectly fine holiday. I do, though.

Acknowledgements

I would like to thank my agents Harriet Moore and David Evans, and my editor Cian McCourt. I am indebted to those who put time into reading and advising on drafts of this novel; Alfie Meadows, Sharon Simpkin, Alexandra Symons-Sutcliffe. Stacy Skolnik, who has been reading it from the very beginning, deserves special thanks. As does Joe Walsh, without whose infinite patience and stern encouragement this would not have happened at all.

The writing of this book was enabled by grants from the Society of Authors and Arts Council England.